In the
Twinkling
of an Eye

In the Twinkling of an Eye

of an Eye

ABRIDGED & UPDATED

*IMAGINE THE
RETURN OF CHRIST
WITH THIS
GROUNDBREAKING,
THOUGHT-PROVOKING
NOVEL*

SYDNEY WATSON

BARBOUR
PUBLISHING

© 2013 by Barbour Publishing, Inc.

Editorial assistance by Jill Jones.

Print ISBN 978-1-62029-768-1

eBook Editions:
Adobe Digital Edition (.epub) 978-1-62416-074-5
Kindle and MobiPocket Edition (.prc) 978-1-62416-073-8

Cover image © Shutterstock/Richard Schramm

Published by Barbour Publishing, Inc., P.O. Box 719, Uhrichsville, Ohio 44683, www.barbourbooks.com

Our mission is to publish and distribute inspirational products offering exceptional value and biblical encouragement to the masses.

Member of the
Evangelical Christian
Publishers Association

Printed in the United States of America.

Contents

Introduction

Long before there was *Left Behind*, there was *In the Twinkling of an Eye*.

Beginning in the mid-1990s, Tim LaHaye and Jerry Jenkins spun a series of end-times novels that captured the imagination of both Christians and the major media—as their *Left Behind* books regularly reached the *New York Times* bestseller lists and were adapted into three full-length feature films.

But some eighty years earlier, Sydney Watson's end-times trilogy paved the way for *Left Behind*. In 1910, *In the Twinkling of an Eye* was published, after "simmering and seething" in Watson's mind for several years. "The first and only real problem I had to face in the matter," he wrote in the book's original preface, "was that of the *principle* involved in using the fictional form to clothe so sacred a subject (for, to me, the near Return of our Lord is the *most* sacred of all subjects)."

That issue settled, however, Watson went on to pen *In the Twinkling of an Eye* and two sequels, *Scarlet and Purple* and *The Mark of the Beast*, throughout the teens. Watson wrote that his goal was to " 'startle' and awaken 'careless, ill-taught professing Christians,' by giving some faint view of the fate of those professors who will be 'left behind' to go through the horrors of The Tribulation."

This perspective on the Rapture takes place in turn-of-the-twentieth-century London, England. In the story, journalist Tom Hammond witnesses the shocking rapture of the Church and its aftermath. What happens when thousands of Christians simply disappear? Why are some people taken while others remain?

Fast-paced, exciting, and thought-provoking, this edition of *In the Twinkling of an Eye* has been lightly abridged and updated for modern readers, and specially typeset for optimal reading.

Chapter 1

❧

TAKEN AT THE FLOOD

The man walked aimlessly through the pressing crowd. He was moody and stern. His eyes showed his disappointment and perplexity. At times, about his mouth there lurked an almost savage expression. As a rule he stood and walked erect like a soldier, but today there was nothing of the soldier in his pose or gait.

It was eleven in the morning. The place was Piccadilly. He came abreast of Swan and Edgar's. The pavement was thronged with women bent on shopping. More than one of them shot an admiring glance at him, for he had the face, the head, of a king among men. But he had not eyes for these chance admirers.

Tom Hammond was thirty years of age, a journalist, and an exceptionally clever one. He was a keen, shrewd man and was gifted with a foresight that was almost remarkable. He had strongly fixed ideas of what a great daily paper should be, but never having seen any attempt that came anywhere close to his ideal, he longed for the time and opportunity when, with practically unlimited capital behind him and a perfectly free hand to use it, he could issue his ideal journal.

This morning he seemed further from the goal of his hopes than ever. For two years he had been subeditor of a London daily that had made for itself a great name—of sorts. There were certain reasons that had prompted him to hope, to expect, the actual editorship before long. But now his house of cards had suddenly tumbled about his ears.

A change had recently taken place in the composition of the syndicate that financed the journal. There were wheels within wheels, and in their whirling they had suddenly produced unexpected results. The editor-in-chief had resigned, and the newly elected editor proved to be a man who had, years before, done Tom the foulest wrong one journalist can do to another.

Under the present circumstance there had been no honorable course open for Tom but to resign. That morning he had found his resignation not only accepted, but himself practically dismissed.

To escape the crowd that almost blocked the pavement in front of Swan and Edgar's windows, he turned sharply into the road and ran into the arms of a young man.

"Tom Hammond!"

"George Carlyon!"

The greeting flew simultaneously from the lips of the two men. They gripped hands.

"By all that's wonderful!" cried Carlyon, still wringing his friend's hand. "Do you know, Tom, I am actually up here in town for one purpose only—to hunt you up."

"To hunt me up!"

"Oh, let's get out of this crush, old man," interrupted Carlyon.

The pair steered their way through the traffic then struck across to the Avenue. In the comparative lull of that walk, Carlyon went on:

"Yes, I've run up to town this morning to find you out and ask you one question: Are you too fixed up with your present newspaper to forbid your entertaining the thought of a real plum in the journalistic market?"

Tom perked up and cried excitedly, "Don't keep me in suspense, Carlyon; tell me quickly what you mean."

"Let's jump into a cab, Tom. I can talk better as we ride."

Carlyon had caught the eye of a cabdriver, and the next moment the two friends were being driven along toward the river. He caught the impatient look on Tom's face and with a light laugh said, "You're on thorns, old boy, to hear about the journalistic plum. Well, here goes. You once met my uncle, Sir Archibald Carlyon?"

Tom nodded.

"He is crazy to start a daily," said Carlyon. "It is no new craze with him; he has been itching to do it for years. And now that gold has been discovered on that land of his in western Australia, and he is likely to be a multimillionaire, now that he is rich beyond all his dreams, he won't wait another day; he will be a newspaper proprietor.

"He wants to find at once a good journalist who is also a keen businessman, one who will take hold of the whole thing. To the right man he will give a perfectly free hand, will interfere with nothing, but be content simply to finance the affair."

An almost fierce light was burning in the eyes of the eager, listening Tom. A thousand thoughts rioted through his brain, but he uttered no word; he would not interrupt his friend.

"I told Nunkums last night—that is what I call him—that I had heard you say it was easier to drop a hundred or two hundred thousand pounds over the starting of a new paper than perhaps over any other venture in the world.

"Nunkums just smiled as I spoke, dropped a walnut into his port glass, and said quietly, 'Then I'll drop them.'

"He hooked that walnut out of his wine with a miniature silver boat hook, devoured the wine-saturated nut, then smiled back into my face as he said: 'Yes, Georgie, I am quite prepared to drop my hundred, two hundred, three hundred thousand, if need be, as I did my walnut. But I am equally hopeful—if I can secure the right man to edit and manage my paper—that I shall eventually hook out an excellent dividend for my outlay. I want a man who not only knows how to do his own work well, as an editor, but one who has the true instinct in choosing his staff.'

"Of course, Tom, I trotted you out before him. He remembered you, of course, and jumped at the idea of getting you, if you were to be got. The upshot of it is, nothing would satisfy him but that I should come up by an early train this morning. Now, tell me, are you open to meet with Sir Archibald?"

"Yes, and can begin business this very day!" Tom laughed with the abandon of a boy as he told, in a few sentences, the story of his dismissal.

"Good!" Carlyon slapped his friend's knee.

"Sir Archibald," he went on, "was to come up by the 10:05 from our place, due at Waterloo at 11:49. He'll be fixed up at the hotel by this time. That's where we are driving now, and—ah! Here we are!"

A moment later the two men were mounting the hotel steps. One of the servants standing in the vestibule recognized Carlyon and saluted him.

"My uncle arrived, Bates?" Carlyon asked.

"Yes, sir, and a young lady with him!"

Carlyon turned quickly to Hammond.

"That's Madge, my American cousin, Tom. I'm awfully glad she has come; I should like you to know her."

Three steps at a time, laughing and talking all the

while, Carlyon raced up the staircase, followed more slowly by his friend.

Tom never wholly forgot the picture of the sitting room and its occupant as he entered with Carlyon. The room was a large one, exquisitely furnished and flooded with a warm, mellow light. A small but cheerful-looking wood fire burned on the tiled hearth, the atmosphere of the room fragrant with a soft, subtle odor, as though the burning wood were scented. From a couch, as the two men entered, a girl rose briskly and faced them. The warm, mellow light that filled the room seemed to clothe her as she stood to meet them. "America" was stamped upon her and her dress, upon the arrangement of her hair, upon the very droop of her figure. She was tall, fair, with that exquisite coloring and smoothness of complexion that is the product of a healthy, hygienic life.

Her face could not be pronounced wholly beautiful, but it was a face that was full of life and charm, her eyes being especially arresting.

"Awfully glad you came up, Madge!" cried Carlyon. "I've run my quarry down. This is Tom Hammond."

He made a couple of mockingly funny elaborate bows, saying: "Miss Madge Finisterre, of Duchess County, New York. Mr. Tom Hammond, of—of everywhere, of London just at present."

Tom bowed to the girl. She returned his salute and then held forth her hand in a frank, pleasant way as she laughingly said, "I have heard so much of Tom

Hammond during the last few days that I guess you seem like an old acquaintance."

Tom shook hands with the maiden, and for a moment or two they chatted as freely and merrily as though they were old acquaintances.

The voice of Carlyon broke into their chat, asking, "Where's Nunkums, Madge?"

Before the girl could reply, the door opened and Sir Archibald entered the room.

One glance into his face would have been sufficient to have told Tom the type of man he had to deal with, even if he had not seen him before. A warmhearted, unconventional, impulsive man, a perfect gentleman in appearance, but a merry, hail-fellow-well-met man in his dealings with his fellow man.

With a bit of mock drama in the gesture, Madge Finisterre flourished her hand toward the newcomer, crying, "Sir Archibald, George? Lo, he is here!"

George made the introductions then the three men passed through the doorway and made for the study-like room of Sir Archibald.

Chapter 2

❧

THE COURIER

For two hours the three men held close conference together. At the end of that time, all the preliminaries of the new venture were settled. Tom had explained his long-cherished views of what the ideal daily paper should be. Sir Archibald was delighted with the scheme and gave Tom a perfectly free hand.

"You were on the point of saying something about a striking poster to announce the coming paper, Mr. Hammond," said the old baronet.

"Yes," Tom replied. "I think a great deal may be done by grabbing the attention of the people—those in London especially. My idea for a poster is this: The name of the paper is to be *The Courier*. Let us have an immense sheet poster, first-class drawing, and bold, attention-getting title of the paper and announcement of its issue. Following the title, I would have in the extreme left a massive signpost, a prominent arm of the structure bearing the legend 'Tomorrow.' On the extreme right of the picture I would put another signpost, the arm of which would bear the words 'The Day After Tomorrow.' I would have a splendidly drawn mounted courier, the horse galloping toward the right-hand post, having left 'Tomorrow' well in the rear."

The old baronet exclaimed, "Rush the thing on! Flood the billboards of all the large towns, and the smaller ones as well, if you can get billboards big enough. Don't worry about the expense, either in the getup or in the issue of the picture."

The old man sprang to his feet and paced the floor, rubbing his hands. "Good! Good! We'll wake old England up. We'll—"

"Toddle into lunch," interrupted George Carlyon.

Tom sat next to Madge at luncheon and was charmed with her easy, unconventional manners. But his mind was too full of the new paper, of the great opportunity that had come to him so unexpectedly, to be as wholly absorbed with the charm of her personality as he might otherwise have been.

He did not linger over the luncheon table.

"There are one or two fellows, Sir Archibald," he explained, "whom I should like to secure on my staff at once. I don't want to lose even an hour."

As he bade Madge Finisterre good-bye, he expressed the hope that he might see her again soon, and the girl in reply allowed her eyes to unconsciously express more than her words.

"She is the most charming woman I ever met," he told himself as he followed Sir Archibald into his room for a final word for which the baronet had asked. George Carlyon had remained behind with Madge.

After discussing the terms of Tom's pay, there were a few more words exchanged between master and man, and then they parted.

As Tom strode along the Embankment toward Waterloo Bridge, his heart was the heart of a boy again. "Is life worth living!" he cried inwardly, answering his own question with the rapturous words: "In this hour I know nothing else that earth could give me to make life more joyous!"

He moved forward in a strange rapture of spirit. He was momentarily unconscious how he traveled or where. He might have been blind or deaf for all that he now saw or heard. The drone of a blind beggar's voice reciting the scriptures, however, presently had power to break his trance. He paused a moment before the man.

"This same Jesus," droned the blind man's voice, "who was taken up from you into heaven, will so come in like manner as you saw Him go into heaven."

Tom dropped a sixpence into the beggar's box and moved away, the wonder of the words he had just heard reciting eclipsing all his previous thoughts of his success.

"Will so come in like manner!" he murmured. "I wonder what it means?"

Chapter 3

&

FLOTSAM

"Only nine hours!"

Tom laughed amusedly at his own murmured thought. It seemed ridiculous almost to try to believe that only nine hours before he had been a discharged journalist, while now he was at the head of what he knew would be the greatest journalistic venture London had ever seen.

He had just dined. He felt that he wanted some kind of movement, some distraction, to relieve the tension. Some instinct turned his feet riverward.

It was now a quarter past seven o'clock. Night had fallen on London. The heavier traffic of London's commercial life had almost ceased. The omnibuses going west were filled with theatergoers and other pleasure seekers. Cabs flitted swiftly either way.

He moved onward in the direction of the law courts. Soon he neared the Waterloo Bridge approach.

He had, without realizing it, been walking toward the river. A moment or two later and he was leaning on the parapet of the bridge, looking down into the dark waters. Sluggish, oil-like in appearance, as seen in the dull gleam of the lamps, the river moved seaward. A sudden longing to get out upon those dark waters came to him.

"If only—" he mused. Then, turning briskly, he came face-to-face with a man in a blue woolen shirt who was crossing the bridge. It was the very man of his half-muttered thought. "If only I could run up against Bob Carter!" he had almost said.

"Good evening, Mister Ham'nd," the man saluted with a thick, tar-stained forefinger as he recognized Tom.

"Good evening, Carter." Tom laughed as he added, "I was just wishing I could meet you, for I felt I should like to get out on the river."

"I'm jes' going as fur as Bambeff, sir. Ef yer likes ter go wif me, you'll do me proud, sir; yer know that, I knows!"

A few minutes later the two men sat in Carter's boat. Tom, in the stern, was steering. Carter manipulated the oars. The man was ordinarily a silent companion, and tonight after a few exchanged words between the pair, he was as silent as usual.

Down the wide, turgid river the boat, propelled by Carter's two oars, shot jerkily.

Tom enjoyed the silence. There was a weirdness about this night trip on the river that fit his mood.

His brain had been considerably overwrought that day. The quiet row was beginning to soothe the nerves.

"Shh!" Carter hissed. Tom saw that his face was turned shoreward. He heaved aft toward Tom and whispered, "Kin yer see that woman, sir?" He jerked his chin in the direction of a line of moored barges.

Tom had turned his head and could plainly discern the form of a woman standing on the edge of the outer barge of the cluster.

The men in the boat sat still, but watchful.

"Do she mean sooerside, sir?" whispered Carter. "Looks like it, sir. Don't make a soun'."

Even as he spoke the woman leaped into the air. There was a low scream, a splash, a leap of foam flashed dully for one instant, then all was still again.

The waterman plied his oars furiously. Tom steered for the spot where that foam had splashed. An instant later the boat was over the place where the body had disappeared. Carter lay on his oars and peered into the darkness on one side. Tom strained his eyes on the other side.

With startling suddenness a hand darted within a foot of where Hammond sat in the stern of the boat. In the same instant the woman's head appeared. Hammond reached out excitedly and caught the hair of the woman, twisting his fingers securely into the knot of hair at the back of her head.

Carter shipped his oars, and in two minutes the woman was safe in the boat. Her drenched face gleamed white where they laid her. A low whimpering sob broke from her.

"Turn 'er over on her face a little, sir, while I makes the boat fast fur a minute or two," jerked out the waterman. "Pore soul! She 'ave took a bellyful of Thames water, an' it ain't filtered no sort, that's sartin!"

Tom had by this time turned the woman over on her face. Almost instantly the woman was very sick.

"In my locker there, sir, I've got a drop o' whiskey. I keeps it there fur 'mergencies like this," said Carter.

Tom moved to allow the man to reach a seat locker in the stern. The next minute, while Tom supported the woman, the waterman poured a few drops of the whiskey down her throat.

She coughed and sputtered, but the drink restored her. She began to whimper.

"We must get her ashore, Carter," cried Tom. "I'll take the oars, and as you know the riverside better than I do, just steer into the nearest landing place you know."

Carter leaped to the bow, cast off the painter, and hurried aft again.

"Jes' 'long yere, sir, there's an old landin' as'll jes' serve us. Wots yer fink ter do wi' the pore soul, sir— not 'and her over to the perlice?"

"No, neither the police nor workhouse, Carter. I wish I could see her face and see what kind of woman she is."

By way of reply, Carter struck a match and lit a small lantern. When the wick had caught light, he flashed it on the face of the woman.

Her eyes were closed; her face was deadly pale.
Her hair was disheveled. But in the one flash glance
Tom had of her, he recognized her.

"It's Mrs. Joyce!" he muttered half aloud in
amazed tones.

"Know 'er, sir?" asked the waterman.

"A little!" he replied. "Her husband is a
reporter—a drinking scamp."

Carter shut off the light of the lantern.

"We're jes' 'ere now, sir, so's best not be callin'
'tention like wi' a light."

He steered the boat into a kind of narrow alley-
way between two crazy old wharves.

Tom, rightly gauging the kindly heart of his landlady,
had brought the drenched woman in a cab to his
lodgings. She was still in a half-fainting condition
when he carried her into the house. In two sentences
he explained the situation to the landlady, whose
natural kindness and loyalty to her lodger made her
willing to help.

"I will carry her up to the bathroom," he said.
"Let your girl get a cup of milk heated as hot as can
be sipped while you bathe this poor soul quickly in
very hot water. Then put her to bed and have some
good, nourishing soup ready. She'll probably sleep
after that. And in the morning—well, the events of
the morning will take their own shape."

Half an hour later, as Tom took a cup of coffee,
he had the satisfaction of knowing that the woman he

had saved was in bed and doing well.

"Poor soul!" he mused. "That brute of a husband has probably driven her to attempt to take her life."

It was nearly ten now. He had no desire to go out again. It was still two hours till his usual bedtime. But a strange sense of drowsiness began to steal over him, and he went off to his bed.

"What a day this has been!" he muttered as he laid his head on the pillow.

Chapter 4

❧

"I Only Reaped What I Sowed"

Tom awaited the woman whom he had saved from drowning.

"She has slept fairly well," the landlady told him, "and I made her eat a good breakfast that I carried up to her myself, Mr. Hammond!"

Now he waited to speak to her. A moment or two more and the landlady ushered her into the room then slipped away.

"How can I ever repay you, sir!" cried the woman, seizing the hand that Hammond held out for her.

For a moment or two her emotion was too great for further speech. Hammond led her to an armchair and seated her. She sobbed convulsively for a moment or two. He allowed her to sob. Presently tears came. The emotion passed, the tears relieved her, and she lifted her sad, beautiful eyes to his face.

"You know how I came to be in the water. I tried

to take my life. I was miserable, despairing! God forgive me."

His strong eyes were full of a rare tenderness as he said, "But, Mrs. Joyce, you surely know that death is not the end of all existence. I am not what would be called a religious man, but every fiber of my inward being tells me that death does not end all."

He saw a shiver pass over her as she hoarsely replied, "I, too, realized that this morning, Mr. Hammond. But last night the madness of an overwhelming despair was upon me. My life had been a literal hell for years, until yesterday I could bear it no longer. I was famished with hunger, sick with despair, and—"

She sighed wearily. "Perhaps," she went on, "if you knew all I have borne, you would not wonder at my rash, mad act."

"Tell me your story, Mrs. Joyce," he said gently. "It may relieve your overcharged heart, and anyhow, I will be your friend, as far as I can."

She sighed again. This time there was a note of relief in the sigh.

"My father was a well-to-do farmer," she began. "I was the only child, and I fear I was spoiled. I received the best education possible and loved my studies. I had been engaged to a young yeoman farmer for nearly a year. I had known him all my life, and we had been sweethearts even as children. Then there came suddenly into my life that man Joyce, for whom I sacrificed everything. God only knows how he contrived to exercise such an awful fascination over me as to make me leave everyone, everything, and marry him.

"I killed my father by eloping on the very eve of my arranged marriage with Ronald Ferris. Ronald left the country as soon as he could wind up his affairs. And I—well, here in this mighty Babylon, I have ever since been reaping some of the sorrow I had sown. Not a penny of my father's money ever reached me, and that brute Joyce only married me for what he expected to get with me. He has done his best to make earth a hell for me, and I, in my mad blindness last night, almost exchanged earth's fleeting hell for God's eternal hell.

"What you reminded me of just now, Mr. Hammond, I know only too well—that death does not end all. My father was a true Christian and a lay preacher. I have traveled with him hundreds of times to his preaching appointments. More than once the sense of God's claim upon me was so great as almost to compel my yielding my heart and life. I wish I had! But my pride, my ambitions, strangled my good desires, and as I said just now, I broke my father's heart. I killed him and ruined my own life. Then London life, my husband's brutality, my own misery, all helped to drive even the memory of God from my mind."

"Yet," broke in Tom, "the Christian religion teaches that sorrow and suffering ought to drive the possessor of the faith nearer to God."

There was a hint of apology in his tones as he went on: "Don't misunderstand me, Mrs. Joyce; I only speak from hearsay. I have heard parsons preach it, but I know nothing experimentally about these things myself."

She smiled in a slow, sad way and said, "Neither have I ever known anything experimentally of these truths. I drifted into the outward form of a correct, religious life. But of God, of Christ, of the divine life, I fear I knew nothing."

Tom asked with apparent irrelevance, "Where is your husband, Mrs. Joyce?"

"Off on one of his drinking bouts, or maybe locked up for drunkenness; I cannot say."

Her lifted eyes were full of beseeching as she went on: "You will keep secret, Mr. Hammond, all this wild, mad episode of my life. If only I could know that the sad story was locked up between God and you, your kind landlady and myself, I think I could go back and face my misery better."

"Do not fear, Mrs. Joyce," he replied quickly. "The affair shall be as though it had never been. I can answer for Mrs. Belcher, my landlady; and for myself I give you my word, and—"

"God reward you, sir!" she sobbed. "Already you have given me clearer views of Him than any minister or any sermon ever did."

A few moments later Mrs. Joyce rose to leave. He pressed three sovereigns into her hand and, in spite of her tearful protestations, made her take the money.

"If you are ever in desperate need, come to me, write to me, Mrs. Joyce, and I will help you, if I can. Meanwhile, be assured that the little I have done for you I would have done for any stranger. Good-bye."

She wrung the hand he gave her, then with a sudden, impulsive movement, she lifted it to her lips and kissed it with a tearful passion.

The next moment she was gone. His hand was wet with her tears.

"Poor soul!" he muttered.

Passing across the room to the window, he glanced out. She was moving down the street.

Chapter 5

❧

LILY WORK

The room we now enter is a large one. The man there at work pauses for a moment.

The room is a workshop. The man is a Jew—and what a Jew! He might have posed for an artist as a model, a type of the proudest Jewish monarch over Israel. Face, form, stature—not even Saul or David or Solomon could have excelled him.

The room held the finished workmanship of his hands for the past three years. And now, as he paused in his labor for a moment and drew his tall form erect and lifted his face to the window above him, a light that was almost holy filled his eyes.

"God of our fathers," he murmured, "God of the Holy Tent and of the temple, instruct me; teach my fingers to do this great work."

He let his hands fall with an almost sacred touch upon the chapiter, the ornamental capital of a pillar, he had been carving. His face shone with an unearthly light, as for a moment his lips moved in prayer. Then quietly grabbing a thick old book from a shelf, he opened it at one of its earliest pages and read aloud:

" 'Then the Lord spoke to Moses, saying: "See, I have called by name Bezalel the son of Uri, the son of Hur, of the tribe of Judah. And I have filled him with the Spirit of God, in wisdom, in understanding, in knowledge, and in all manner of workmanship, to design artistic works, to work in gold, in silver, in bronze, in cutting jewels for setting, in carving wood, and to work in all manner of workmanship. And I, indeed I, have appointed with him Aholiab the son of Ahisamach, of the tribe of Dan; and I have put wisdom in the hearts of all the gifted artisans, that they may make all that I have commanded you: the tabernacle of meeting, the ark of the Testimony and the mercy seat that is on it, and all the furniture of the tabernacle" ' " (Exodus 31:1–7).

His fingers moved to the middle of the book. Again he read aloud:

"The capitals which were on top of the pillars in the hall were in the shape of lilies . . . The capitals on the two pillars also had pomegranates above. . . and there were two hundred such pomegranates in rows on each of the capitals all around. Then he set up the pillars by the vestibule of the temple; he set up the pillar on the right and called its name Jachin, and he set up the pillar on the left and called its name Boaz. The tops of the pillars were in the shape of lilies. So the work of the pillars was finished" (1 Kings 7:19–22).

With a reverent touch the man closed the book, replaced it on the shelf, then, lifting his eyes again, he murmured: "How long, O Lord, will Your people be cast off and trodden down, and their land, Your land, be held by the accursed races?"

For a moment a look of pain swept across his face. Then, as he became conscious of the touch of his lowered hand upon the chapter, his eyes traveled downward to the exquisite "lily work," and the light of a new hope swept the pain off his face.

"The very fact that the time has come," he murmured, "for us to be preparing for the next temple is a token from Jehovah that the day of Messiah draws near."

His eyes lingered a moment on the rare and beautiful workmanship, and then he took up a carving tool and continued his toil; yet while he worked he kept up a running recitative of Ezekiel's description of the great temple—for he knew by heart all the chapters of that prophet.

In the midst of his rapt devotion, the door of the workroom opened. The slight sound aroused the dreamer. He turned his face in the direction of the door, and his eyes flashed with pleasure.

"Ah, Zillah!" he cried in greeting. The girl he addressed closed the door. She crossed the floor quickly, with a certain eagerness, and came toward him with a rare grace. She was singularly beautiful, of an Eastern style of beauty. Her complexion was of the Spanish olive tone, and her melting eyes were of that same Spanish type. Her wondrous hair was blue-black. She had a certain plumpness of form that seemed to add rather than detract from her general beauty. She was his wife's sister.

"Supper will be ready in five minutes, Abraham," she began. "Will you be ready for it?"

He smiled down into her great black eyes. He was never very keen on his meals. He ate to live only; he did not live to eat. She knew that and had long since learned that his labor of love was as meat and drink to him. Her eyes glided past him and rested on his work.

"It is very beautiful, Abraham!" she cried. There was reverence as well as rapture and admiration in her voice and glance.

"It cannot be too beautiful, Zillah," he returned.

"When will the Messiah come?" she sighed.

"Soon, I believe!" he returned. "Jehovah rested in His creative work after six days' labor. A thousand years with Him are as one day. May it not well be, then, that as there have passed nearly six thousand years—each thousand years representing one day—that He will presently rest in His finished work for His people, through the coming of the Messiah, as He did at the creation?"

He laid his tool aside and turned to the girl as he continued: "Besides, do not our sacred books say that when three springs have been discovered on Mount Zion, Messiah will come? Two springs have lately been discovered by the excavators in Jerusalem, and our people out there excitedly watch the work of these men, expecting soon the discovery of the third spring."

Her eager, parted lips told how she hung upon his speech. He smiled down gratefully into her eyes, though a sigh escaped him as he said, "Ah! I wish Leah would only show a little of the interest in all this that you do, Zillah!"

"You must not blame Leah too much, Abraham," the girl answered quickly. "She has her children, you know. Mother always said that if ever Leah had babies, there would be nothing else in the world for her except the babies. Besides, Abraham, no two of us are constituted alike, and Leah is what the Gentiles about here call happy-go-lucky. But, Abraham, tell me more of what you think of Messiah's coming. Leah's five minutes will be sure to run to a quarter of an hour."

"I do think Messiah is coming soon," cried the young fellow excitedly. "Who knows? Perhaps when the Passover comes again, and we set His chair and open the door for Him to enter, that He shall suddenly come."

There was a sudden clatter of little feet outside, and a boy and a girl burst into the room.

"What do you think, Father?" cried the boy. "A boy—he's a Gentile, of course—whom I know says that Messiah has come, that the cursed Nazarene was He, and that—"

"We will go to supper, Reuben, and you and I will talk about that another time." Cohen spoke quietly to his boy. He had his own reasons for checking the subject at that time.

His aunt caught the boy's hand and danced with him out of the room. Rachel, the little girl, clung to her father, and the whole family trooped off to wash their hands before the meal.

Chapter 6

❧

AN INTERESTING TALK

The *Courier* was now an established fact. As a newspaper it was as much a revelation to the journalists as to the general public. London had taken to it from its first issue. The provinces, instead of following their usual course of waiting to see what London did, took their own initiative and adopted the new paper at once. Every instinct about the ideal paper cultivated during Tom's waiting years had been true instinct. He had always felt them to be true; now he realized the fact. He was a proud, happy man.

One curious feature of the new journal had attracted much attention, even before the publication of the first issue. In his "Foreword," as he had termed it, in a full-page announcement that appeared in three of the leading London dailies, Tom had said:

"An important feature of the *Courier* will be the item or items (as the case may be) that will be found each day under the heading 'From the Prophet's Chamber.' A greater man than the editor of the *Courier* once said, 'Every editor of a newspaper ought to have a strain of the seer in his composition. He ought to have the gift of prophecy up to a certain point. He ought to be so thoroughly conversant with the history of his own and every other nation that when history is on the point of repeating itself—as it has a habit of doing—he may not be caught altogether napping.' It is the unexpected that happens, we say.

"True, but there are many of the so-called happenings of the unexpected that to the spirit of the seer will have been expected and more than half prophesied.

"Now, while we propose that the whole tone of the *Courier* will show the spirit of the seer in a measure, we shall endeavor to make the particular column to which we are now alluding essentially new. In it we shall deal with every class of subject likely to prove mentally engaging to our readers and will make it prophetic up to the limits of our capacities as man, citizen, and editor. How far the possession of the quality of the seer will be found in us we must leave the future—and our readers—to decide. But we certainly anticipate that the 'Prophet's Chamber' column will be one of the most popular features of what we shall aim to make the most popular paper of the day."

Tom was no believer in luck. He had left nothing to chance in the production of his paper. There was not a department left to subordinates that he did not personally assure himself was being carried out on the best lines.

He saw very little of Sir Archibald Carlyon during these weeks and nothing at all of George or the fair American, Madge Finisterre. George was in Scotland, Madge on the Continent.

His thoughts often turned to the American girl, and his eye brightened and his pulse quickened when ever he heard of her from Sir Archibald. This morning, he had been reminded of her, and he laid down his pen a moment as he gave himself up to a little reverie about her. An announcement aroused him.

"Miss Finisterre and Mr. Carlyon, sir."

He smiled to himself. "Speaking of angels," he mused.

The next moment he was greeting his callers. Madge Finisterre looked, in Tom's eyes, more radiant now than ever.

"Fancy, Mr. Hammond," she laughed, when the greetings were over, "George and I met at Dover! He had come south to see a friend off from Dover and was on the pier when I landed from the Calais boat. We've been down to that dear old country house, but I wanted to do some shopping and to see how you looked as editor-in-chief and general boss of the biggest daily paper in the world."

Tom's eyes flashed with a pleased light at her words, which implied that she had thought of him, even as he had thought of her. He noted, too, how an extra shade of color warmed the clear skin of her cheeks.

"Because," she went on, "all the world declares that the *Courier* is the premier paper of the world, and everyone who is anyone knows that Mr. Tom Hammond is the *Courier*."

George Carlyon got up from his seat, saying, "I say, you two, do you mind if I leave you to amuse each other for an hour? I want very much to run down to the club. I'll come back for you, Madge, or meet you somewhere."

Madge and Tom assured George they would be fine without him, and George left the room.

It was a strangely new experience to Tom to be left alone with a beautiful and charming woman like Madge Finisterre.

The picture she made, as she moved around the room looking at the framed paintings, came to him with a kind of revelation. When he had met her that day in the Embankment hotel, he had been charmed with her beauty and her frank, open, unconventional manner. He had thought of her many times since, thought of her as men think of a picture or a poem that has given them delight. But now he found her appealing to him.

She was a woman, a beautiful, attractive woman. She suggested sudden thoughts of how a woman, loved and returning that love, might affect his life, his happiness.

Her physical grace and beauty, the exquisite fit

of her costume, the perfect harmony of it—all this struck him now. But the woman in her appealed strongest to him.

"Do you know, Mr. Hammond," she said as she finally seated herself in an armchair, "I just wanted very much to see how you were fixed up here and how you looked now that you are a big man."

He made a deprecatory little gesture.

"Oh, but you are a really great man," she went on. "I have heard some big people talk of you and say—" She leaned back and smiled merrily at him as she went on: "Well, I guess if there's only a shadow of truth in the old saying, then your ears must often have burned. And I must say I do like *The Courier* immensely, Mr. Hammond," she cried in a tone of warm admiration.

"Thank you, Miss Finisterre!" His eyes said more than his words. "What do you especially like in it? Or is your liking of a more general character?"

"I do like it from a general standpoint," she replied. "I think it's the best paper in the world. But especially do I like your own particular column, 'From the Prophet's Chamber.' But, Mr. Hammond, about the Jew—you are going in strong for him, aren't you?"

"From the ordinary newspaper point, yes," he said. "I cannot quite recall how my mind was first switched on to the subject, but I do know this—that the more I study the past history of the race and the future predictions concerning it, the more amazed I am how, past, present, and future, the Jews, as a nation, are interwoven with everything political, musical, artistic—everything, in fact. And I wonder, equally, that we journalists as a whole should have thought and written so little about them.

"Take their ubiquitousness, Miss Finisterre. There does not appear to have been an empire in the past that has not had its colony of Jews. By which I do not mean a ghetto, a herding of sordid living, illiterate Hebrews, but a sturdy colony of men and women who, by sheer force of intellect, have obtained and maintained the highest positions, the greatest influence."

Madge listened with rapt interest. The man before her talked marvelously.

"It is not simply that they practically hold the wealth of the world in their hands, that they are the world's bankers, but they are dominating our press, our politics."

With glowing words he poured out a flood of wondrous fact and illustration, winding up with: "Then you cannot kill the Jew; you cannot wipe him out. The life of the Hebrew is indestructible. Sometimes of late I have asked myself this question, as I have reviewed the history of the dealings of so-called Christianity with the Semitic race: Has Christianity been afraid of the Jews, or why has she sought to stamp them out?"

The pair had been so engrossed in their talk that they had lost all track of time. Over a half hour had slipped by since George had left them.

"But excuse me, Miss Finisterre, what about some tea? Shall we go out and get some, or would you prefer that I should order it in here?"

"Oh, here, by all means! I can have teas at a restaurant every day of my life, but with a real London lion—a real-life editor—and in his own special den. Why, it may never fall to my lot again. Oh, here, by all means!"

He squeezed a rubber bulb on his desk. To the lad Charlie, who appeared, he gave a written order to a neighboring restaurant. Twenty minutes later the tea was in the room.

Madge officiated with the teapot. Hammond watched her every movement. A truly pretty, graceful girl never looks handsomer to a man than when presiding at a tea table. Tom thought Madge had never looked more charming. The meal was a very enjoyable one, and as she poured out his second cup, he paid her a pretty compliment, adding: "To see you thus, Miss Finisterre, makes one think what fools men are not to—"

He paused abruptly. She flashed a quick glance of inquiry at him.

"Not to what, Mr. Hammond?"

"I wonder," he replied, "if I ought to say what I left unsaid."

"Why not?" she asked.

"I don't know why I should not." He laughed. "I was going to say that to have a bright, beautiful, graceful woman like Madge Finisterre pouring out tea for him makes a man think what a fool he is not to marry."

His tone and glance were both full of meaning. She could not mistake him. Her color heightened visibly. Her eyes drooped before his ardent gaze. The situation became tense and full of meaning.

The opening of the door at that instant changed everything. George had returned. At the same moment a wire was brought to Hammond, together with the afternoon mail.

Chapter 7

რ

"Coming"

George's entrance, the arrival of the afternoon mail, and the telegram gave Madge an opportunity to escape. George was anxious to leave, and Madge rose at once to accompany him.

Tom did not press them to stay, for he, too, felt awkward. The friends shook hands. The eyes of Madge and Tom met for one instant. Each face flushed under the power of the other's glance.

When the door had closed upon them, Tom went back to his old place by the table, his eyes involuntarily sweeping the whole room. He smiled as he suddenly realized how empty the room now seemed.

Tom gathered up his mail and dropped into his seat.

For a full five minutes he sat still thinking, reviewing all the circumstances of the situation the unexpected coming of George Carlyon had interrupted. He asked himself whether he was really in love with the fair Madge and whether he would have proposed to her if her cousin had not so unexpectedly turned up. He made no definite reply to his own question but turned to his mail.

The telegram he had opened at once on its receipt. He turned now to the letters. He had opened all but two. The last one was addressed in a woman's handwriting. Breaking the envelope, he took out the letter and turned first to the signature on the fourth page.

"Millicent Joyce," he read. "Millicent Joyce?" he repeated. Unconsciously he had laid his emphasis on the "Millicent," and he forgot the "Joyce."

But suddenly it came to him that the letter was from Mrs. Joyce, the woman whom he had helped save from drowning on the night of that memorable day when the great chance of his life had come to him.

"Poor soul!" he muttered. "I wonder what she has written about." The next instant he was reading the letter.

Tom cast his eyes over the letter Mrs. Joyce had sent him.

Dear Sir,

I gave you my word that if ever I was in special trouble or need, I would write or come to you for help.

I did not promise you, however, that if any great joy or blessing should come to me that I would let you know. I don't think I believed any joy could ever possibly come into my life again. But joy and wondrous gladness have come into my life, and in an altogether unexpected way.

You will remember how I said to you in parting that your strong, cheery words had given me a clearer view of God than any sermon I had ever listened to. That impression deepened rather than diminished when I got home. My husband, I heard, had been sent to Wandsworth Prison for a month, for assaulting the police when drunk.

And in this month of quiet from his brutalities, the great joy of my life came to me. I began to attend religious services from the very first night after my return home.

One night I went to the hall of the Mission for Railway Men. A lady was speaking that night, and God found me and saved me. All that I had ever heard from my dear father's lips, when he preached about conversion, came back to me, and that night I passed from death to life.

The subject of the address was "The Coming of the Lord." I listened in amazement as the lady speaker declared that, for this age, God evidently meant that this truth of the near coming of Christ should have almost, if not quite, the most prominent place in all public preaching.

I was startled to hear her say that there were nearly three hundred direct references to the second coming of Christ in the Gospels and Epistles, and that there were thus more than double the number of references to that subject than even to that of salvation through the blood of the Atonement.

One thing she said led me to an immediate decision for Christ. She said, "How often is the possibility of sudden death advanced by a preacher as an incentive to unsaved souls to yield to God!

"But how poor an argument is that compared with the near approach of Christ! Sudden death might come to one person in a congregation before twenty-four hours, but in a sense, that would touch that one person only. But if Christ came to take up His people from the earth—the dead in Christ from their graves, the living from their occupations, etc.—this would affect every unsaved soul in every part of the country, of the world, even."

I gave myself up to God there and then, Mr. Hammond, and am seeking now to live so that, should Christ come, even before I finish this letter, I may be ready to be caught up to meet Him in the air.

Hammond paused in his reading.

"What can the woman mean?" he murmured. His

eyes became fixed on space; his mind was searching for something that he had recently heard or read on this strange topic. The clue seemed almost within grasp, yet for a while he could not recall it.

Suddenly it came to him. Like a voice nearby, the drone of that blind beggar's reading came to him, as he had heard it that day on the Embankment.

"This same Jesus, who was taken up from you into heaven, will so come in like manner as you saw Him go into heaven."

"I remember," he mused, "how that sentence caught my attention. My mind was utterly pre-occupied a moment before, but that wondrous sentence pierced my preoccupation."

Tom's face was full of a strange, new perplexity. "Do you know Joyce, Mr. Simpson?" Tom called out to a reporter passing his office. "He used to be on the staff of the—"

"*Daily Tattler*," cried the man. "Knew him well years ago, sir. Old schoolfellows, in fact. Got wrong in the drink, sir. Gone to the dogs, and—"

"Have you seen or heard anything of him this last month, Mr. Simpson?"

"Yes, sir. He's grown worse than ever. Magistrate at Bow Street committed him for three days, said fellow ought to be put in Broadmoor. Pity his poor wife, sir."

"You know Mrs. Joyce, then?" Hammond queried.

The reporter sighed. "Rather, sir! Wished a thousand times I could have had her for a wife, and he'd had mine. I should have had a happier life. And he—" The man laughed grimly. "Well, he'd have had a Tartar!"

Hammond had heard something about the shrewish wife Simpson had unfortunately married. But he had learned all he wanted to know, so he dismissed the poor, ill-married fellow.

"I think I must call upon Mrs. Joyce and learn more about this strange matter of the coming Christ," he told himself.

He copied the address from the head of the letter into his pocketbook then turned to the last letter of his mail.

This proved to be a comparatively short letter but to Hammond, a deeply interesting one. It was signed "Abraham Cohen," and the writer explained that he was a Jew who had taken *The Courier* from the very first number and had not only become profoundly interested in the recent utterances of the editor in the "Prophet's Chamber" column, but he had, for some days, been impressed with the desire to write to the "Prophet."

> *Will you pardon me, sir, if I say that it would*
> *be to your immense advantage, now that your*
> *mind has become aroused to the facts and*
> *history of our race, if you would get in touch*
> *with some really well-read, intelligent Jew who*
> *knows our people well, knows their history,*
> *past, present, and future, as far as the latter*

can be known from our scriptures and sacred books. Should you care to fall in with my suggestion, I should be pleased to supply you with the names and addresses of several good and clever men of our people.

Yours obediently,
Abraham Cohen

As he folded the letter slowly, Hammond told himself that there was something in the letter that drew him toward the writer.

"I will hunt him up, for it is evident that he is as enthusiastic over his people's history as he is intelligent. I will see what tomorrow brings. Now to work."

He put Cohen's letter in his pocket and turned to the hundred and one editorial claims upon his time.

Chapter 8

❧

REVERIE

In spite of the time of year, the evening was almost as warm as one in June. Madge Finisterre was on one of the wide hotel balconies overlooking the Embankment. She had dined with her cousin George, but instead of going out of town that evening with him, she had elected to spend a quiet evening alone.

Her mind was engrossed with the memory of the latter part—the interrupted part—of her meeting with Tom that afternoon.

"What would have happened if George had not turned up at that moment," she mused, "if we had been left alone and undisturbed another five minutes?"

Her cheeks burned as she whispered softly to herself: "I believe Tom Hammond would have proposed to me. If he had, what should I have replied?"

A faraway look crept into her eyes. She was back again in the little town where she had been raised. Her mind flitted swiftly to a scene that had been hanging in the background of her thoughts.

There had been a donation party for their pastor at the house of one of the members. Madge had gone, of course. Some were in the habit of saying that a donation party simply could not be run without her. Things had been a bit stiff and formal at first, as they often are at such gatherings.

The adults had sat around and talked on current topics. The young folk had been moping around. Then Madge had burst upon the scene. She swam into the largest room, swirling round and round with a kind of waltz movement, to the accompaniment of her own gay voice singing a lively tune.

With a gay laugh she had turned to the hostess, saying, "Things want hustling a bit here, Miss Julie. Everyone is as glum as a whippoorwill that is fixed up with the grippe."

She had started the young people playing their favorite games in two or three of the smaller rooms then had raced away again to the room where the adults were sitting squarely against the wall, as grim as bronze images. Dropping on the piano stool, she struck a few soft, tender notes, suggestive of some gracious hymn, then suddenly broke into a lively, raucous song.

Behind a corner of the curtain, the young pastor had watched and listened. He had thought his presence unknown to her. He was mistaken.

For three-quarters of an hour, she had been the life of that room. Then, suddenly, as she was singing at the piano, the room grew very quiet. She was aroused by a voice just behind her ear, saying: "Miss Finisterre, are you going to supper with this first batch, or will you wait till the next turn?"

Turning, she found herself face-to-face with the young pastor, the room being otherwise empty. His gaze was very warm, very ardent. She had flushed under the power of that gaze.

She had railed him on his extra seriousness, and he had answered, "Don't, Madge! You must know why I am grave and sad tonight." (He had never called her Madge before.)

"No, I don't," she had replied.

"In less than a week," he went on, "so I have heard tonight, you leave Balhang. You are going to Europe and will be away long months, perhaps a year."

She had gazed at him in honest wonder, not fully grasping his meaning.

"Why," she asked, "should that make you sad?"

He had leaned closer toward her. There was no one to see them. The heavy door curtain had slipped from its hook and shut them in. Where her hand rested on the rounded, polished arm of the piano, his large hand had moved, and her white fingers were clasped in his large ones. His eyes had sought hers, and under the hypnotic power of the strong love in his eyes, she had been compelled to meet his gaze.

"I thought, dear, you must have seen how, for a long time, I had learned to love you, Madge."

His clasp on her fingers had tightened. He had leaned nearer to her still. She felt the warmth of his breath, the heat of his clean, wholesome flesh.

Tonight she heard again the pleading voice as he had cried: "Madge, my darling! Can you ever guess how great is my love for you? Tell me, dear, do you, can you, love me in return? Will you be my wife? Will you come into my life to bless it? And let me be wholly yours to help, to bless, to strengthen, to love, to cherish you? Tell me, darling!"

And she had cried: "I don't know how to answer you, Pastor. It is all so sudden. I knew, of course, that we were great friends, and I am sure I like you very much, but—this proposal! Why, I never dreamed that you cared for me like that, for how could I be a minister's wife? I am such a gay, thoughtless, foolish little thing—I—"

There had followed more tender pleading, and she had finally said, "If you love me, Homer, as you say you do, please do not bother me anymore now. Wait until I come back from Europe—then—then— if I can honestly say yes, I will, and I will not even wait for you to ask me again."

He had bent over her. His gaze held her fascinated. She thought he was going to take toll of her lips before his right was confirmed. But at that instant there had come a rush of feet, a sound of many voices. The curtain was flung aside, just as her fingers strayed over the keys of the instrument, and the pastor succeeded in regaining his old unseen nook.

Except for one moment, when she was leaving the house for home and he had helped her on with her cloak, the pastor had not spoken again directly to her that evening. He had managed then to whisper, "God bless you, my darling! I shall pray for you, and live on the hope I read in your eyes tonight."

It was all this that had risen so strangely before her mind tonight on that hotel balcony as she had begun to ask herself how much she really cared for Tom Hammond and what answer she would have given him had he proposed to her that afternoon.

"I told Pastor," she murmured, "that night that I was not sure of myself. I am no nearer being sure of myself now than I was then."

The scene with Tom rose up before her, and she added: "I am less sure, I think, than ever!"

For a moment she tried to compare the two lives—that of an American pastor's wife, with endless possibilities of doing good, and that of the wife of a comparatively wealthy newspaper editor-manager.

"Should I like to marry a popular man?" she asked herself. "I read somewhere once that popular men, like popular actors, made bad husbands, that they cannot endure the tameness of an audience of one."

She laughed low as she added: "Oh, well, Tom Hammond has not asked me to marry him. Perhaps he never will."

The night had grown cooler. She shivered a little

as she rose and passed into the lighted room beyond.

Two hours later, as she laid her head upon the pillow, she murmured, "I don't see how I could marry the pastor! Why, I haven't 'got religion' yet. I am not 'converted,' as these Britishers would say!"

Chapter 9

❧

A Threat

Tom paused before the house that bore the number at the head of Mrs. Joyce's letter. It was on a poor, obscure street, and his soul went out to the unfortunate woman who, with all her refinement, was compelled to live amid such squalid surroundings.

A child opened the door in response to his knock. Following the directions given, Tom climbed the dirty stairs. On the top landing were two doors. The one on the right was fast shut; that on the left was ajar a few inches. His approach did not seem to have been heard. Mrs. Joyce, the only occupant of the room, was seated at a bare table, sewing briskly.

He stretched out his hand to tap the door, but some impulse checked him for a moment. He had the opportunity to observe her closely, and he did so.

She sat facing the window; the light shone full upon her. She was dressed in a well-worn but well-fitting black gown. Her hair hung in clustering waves on her neck and was held back behind her ears with a comb on either side. There was a rare softness and refinement in the pale face that drooped over her sewing. Seen as Tom saw her there, Mrs. Joyce was a beautiful woman.

He gazed for a few moments at the picture, amazed at the rapidity of her sewing movements.

Under the magnetic constraint of his fixed gaze, the woman looked toward the door. She recognized her visitor and with a little glad cry started to her feet. Tom pushed the door open and entered the room. She sprang to meet him.

Now that he saw her, he realized the expression of her face had changed. Heaven—all the heaven of God's indwelling pardon, love, peace—had come to dwell with her. All that she had said in her letter of her newfound joy was fully confirmed by her looks.

"How good of you to come to see me, Mr. Hammond!" she cried.

"How good of you to write me of your newfound happiness!" He smiled back into her glad, eager eyes.

He took the chair she offered and with a question or two sought to encourage her to talk about the subject he had come to see her about.

"The very title of the subject," Tom explained, "is perfectly foreign to me."

"It was all so, *so* foreign to me," she returned. Then, as tears flooded her eyes, she said, "And it would all have been foreign to me forever but for *you*, Mr. Hammond. I never, *never* can forget that but for you my soul would have been in a suicide's hell, where hope and mercy could never have reached me. As long as I shall live, I shall never forget the awful rush of soul accusation that swept over me when my body touched the foul waters of that muddy river that night.

"I saw all my life as in a flash. All the gracious warnings and pleadings that ever, in my hearing, fell from my sainted father's lips, as he beseeched men and women to be reconciled to God, seemed to swoop down upon me, condemning me for my unbelief and sin. Then—then you came to my rescue—and—"

Her tears were dropping thick and fast now.

"And—my soul—had respite given in which to—seek God—because—you saved my body."

Overcome with emotion, she turned her head to wipe away the grateful tears. When next she faced him, her voice was low and tender.

"Now, if my Lord come," she said softly, "I shall be ready to meet Him in the air. I used to think that if ever I was converted, I would meet my dear father and mother at the last day, at the great final end of all things.

"But now I know that if Jesus came for His people today, that I would meet my dear ones today."

Tom gazed at the speaker in wonder. "Tell me of this wonderful thing, Mrs. Joyce," he said, "that can transmute your poverty and suffering to triumph and rapture, and your comfortless garret to a heaven on earth."

"Before I begin," she replied, "tell me, Mr. Hammond, have ever you seen this?"

From the window shelf she grabbed a tiny booklet.

"Long Odds!" he said, reading the boldly printed title of the book. "No; I have never seen this."

"Take it, Mr. Hammond," she went on. "If it does nothing else, it will awaken your interest in the wonderful subject."

He slipped the book into his breast pocket. She opened her mouth to speak again when a sound from outside caught her ear. She started to her feet; her face turned deadly pale. The next instant the door was flung noisily open, and her husband entered the room.

The bleary-eyed, drunken scoundrel glared at the two seated figures then laughed evilly as he cried, "Turned religious? Oho! Oho! Like all the rest of your religious people, make a mantle of your religion to cover every blackness and filthiness of life."

"Silence, you foulmouthed blackguard!" Tom's lips were white with the indignation that filled him as he flung his command at the man.

"Silence yourself, Tom Hammond!" bellowed the drunken scoundrel. "I know you. You're a big bug now! Think no end of yourself and of your paper. Perhaps you'll say you came to invite me to join your staff, now that I've caught you here!"

His sneering tone changed to one of bitterest hate as he turned to the white, trembling woman.

"You're a beauty, ain't you? Profess to turn saint, then, when you think I'm clear away, you receive visits from fine gentlemen! Gentlemen? Bah! They're—"

"Silence, you drunken, foulmouthed beast!" again interrupted Tom.

There was something amazing in the command that rang in the indignant tones of his voice.

"Unless," he went on, "you want to find yourself in the grip of the law."

For a moment or two Joyce was utterly cowed! Then the devil in him reared its head again, and he hissed, "You clear out of here, and remember this: If I have to keep sober for a year to do it, I'll ruin you, Tom Hammond, I will!" He laughed with an almost demoniacal glee. "I can write a paragraph yet, you know. I'll dip my pen in the acid of hate and then get Fletcher to put it into his paper. He's not in love with the *Courier*, or with Tom Hammond, the editor."

"You scurrilous wretch!" It was all that Tom deigned to reply.

"Good day, Mrs. Joyce!" He bowed to the white-faced woman.

For her sake he did not offer to shake hands but moved away down the stairs.

He caught a cab a few moments later. He had purposed, when he started out that morning, to hunt up his other correspondent, the Jew, Abraham Cohen. But after the scene he had just witnessed, he felt quite unwilling to interview a stranger.

"I wish," he mused, as he sat back in the cab, "I

had not gone near that poor soul. I am afraid my visit may make it awkward for her."

His eyes darkened as he added: "And even for myself. It will be very awkward if that drunken brute puts his threat into execution—and he *will*, I believe. Innuendo is a glass dagger that, driven into the victim's character, into his heart and then snapped off from the hilt, leaves no clue to the striker of the blow. And a demon like that Joyce, playing into the hands of a cur like Fletcher, may slay a fellow by a printed innuendo, and yet the pair may easily keep outside the reach of the law of libel.

"Then, too, there is this sudden breakdown of Marsden, and for the life of me, I don't know where to look for a fellow whom I could secure at short notice, who is at all fit to be the *Courier's* second in command."

His face had grown moody. His eyes were full of an unaccustomed depression.

"If only," he went on, "Ralph Bastin had been in England and were to be got—" He sighed.

"Where on earth can Ralph be after all these years?" he muttered.

He glanced out of the cab to ascertain his own whereabouts. In two minutes more he would be at the office.

Chapter 10

❧

IN THE NICK OF TIME

As Tom's cab drew up at the office, another one drew up a yard ahead of his. The occupant alighted at the same instant as Tom and glanced in his direction. Both men leaped forward; their hands were clasped in a grip that told of a very warm friendship. Like simultaneous pistol shots there leaped from their separate lips—

"Tom Hammond!"

"Ralph Bastin?"

The friends passed into the great building, arm linked in arm, laughing and talking like holiday schoolboys.

"Not three minutes ago, as I drove along in my cab, I was saying, 'Oh! if only I could lay my hand on Ralph!' "

They were seated by this time in Tom's room.

"Why? What did you want, Tom—anything

special?" the bronzed, traveled Bastin asked.

"Rather, Ralph! My second in command, poor Frank Marsden, has broken down suddenly; it's serious, may even prove fatal, the doctors say. Anyway, he won't be fit—if he recovers at all—for a year or more."

He leaned eagerly toward his friend as he spoke and asked, "Are you open to take the post?"

"Yes."

"When?"

"Tomorrow, if you like!"

"Good!"

Tom stretched his hand out. Bastin grasped it. Then they talked over terms, duties, etc.

"But you, man?" said Tom when the last bit of shop had been talked. "Where have you been? What have you been doing?"

"Busy for an hour, Tom?" Bastin asked by way of reply.

"No!"

"Come round to my diggings, then. We can talk as we go. I will have time to tell you about my adventures. Then, when you get to my hangout, I can introduce you to *her*, the story of my chief adventure, for it concerns her."

Hammond flashed a quick, wondering glance at his friend.

"*Her*!" he said. "Are you married, then?"

"No," laughed Bastin, "but I've adopted a child. But come on, man!"

The pair left the office. In the cab, talking very rapidly, Bastin gave the skeleton sketch of his wanderings.

Tom never forgot the first sight of his friend's adopted child. There was a low grate in the room, a blazing fire of leaping, flaming coals in the grate. Curled up in a deep saddlebag armchair was the loveliest girl-child Hammond had ever seen.

She must have been half asleep, or in a deep reverie, but as the two men advanced into the room, she sprang from the chair and, with eyes gleaming with delight, bounded to meet Bastin. Wrapping her arms around his neck, she crooned softly over him in some tongue of her own.

She was loveliness incarnated. Her eyes, black as coal, were big, round, and wide in their staring wonder at Tom. Her hair was a mass of short curls. She was dark of skin like some Spanish beauty.

Bastin introduced the child. She gave Tom her hand and lifted her wonderful eyes to his, answering his question as to her health in the prettiest of broken English he had ever heard.

A moment or two later the three friends were seated—Tom and Bastin in armchairs opposite each other, the child (Viola, Bastin had christened her) on a low stool between Bastin's knees.

"Shall we use the old lingo—French?" Bastin asked the question in the Bohemian Parisian they had been in the habit of using together years before.

"As you please, Ralph," Tom replied.

"When I was on a little island in La Caribe, I became acquainted with this little Carib maiden. The child became intensely attached to me, and I to her, and we were always together in the daytime.

"When her mother was stung by a deadly scorpion and died, I made the child my care. She has traveled everywhere with me ever since, and you see how fair and sweet she is and how beautifully she speaks our English. She is barely twelve, is naturally gifted, and is the very light of my life."

Then, addressing Viola and relapsing, of course, into English for her sake, he explained who Tom was and that he (Ralph) was going to be associated with him on the same great newspaper.

"Mr. Hammond and you, Viola, must be real good friends," he added.

"Sure, Daddy!" the girl said, smiling. "I like him much already—"

She lifted herself slightly until she rested on her knees and stretched one hand across the hearth rug to Tom; she laid the other in her guardian's as she went on: "Mr. Hammond is good! I know, I know, for his eyes shine true!"

A ripple of merry laughter escaped her as she gazed back into her guardian's face and added:

"But you, Daddy, are always first."

Chapter 11

❧

Long Odds

Tom could not sleep.

"It must be the various excitements of the day," he muttered. His mind trailed off to the scene of the morning. Suddenly he recalled the booklet Mrs. Joyce had given him.

"I'll find that thing and read it," he muttered.

He got out of bed, passed quickly through to his dressing room, found the coat that he had worn that morning, and secured the booklet.

He went back to bed and, lying on his elbow, opened the dainty little printed thing and began to read.

Long Odds

"You don't say so! Where on earth has she gone?"

"I can't say, sir, but it's plain enough she *is* missing. Hasn't been seen since last night when she went up to her room."

I *was* put out, I own; my man on waking me had informed me that the cook was missing; she had gone to bed without anything being noticed amiss and was now nowhere to be found. She was always an odd woman, but a capital cook. What had become of her? The very last sort of person to disappear in this way—a respectable elderly Scotchwoman—really quite a treasure in the country; and the more I thought of it while I dressed, the more puzzled I became. I hardly liked to send for the police; and then again it was very awkward—people coming to dinner that day. It was really too bad.

But I had scarcely finished dressing when in rushed my man again. I do so dislike people being excited, and he was more than excited.

"Please, sir, Mr. Vend has come round to see you; his coachman has gone—went off in the night and hasn't left a trace behind, and they say the gardener's boy is with him."

"Well," said I, "it is extraordinary; tell Mr. Vend I'm coming. No, stay, I'll go at once."

It was really past belief—the three of them! After an hour's talk with Vend, no explanation offered itself, so we decided to go to town as usual.

We walked down to the station and saw at once something was wrong. Old Weeks, the stationmaster, was quite upset: his pointsman was missing, and the one porter had to take up his duty. However, the train was coming up; we had no time to question him but jumped in. There were three other people in the compartment and I thought I was going off my head when I heard what they were discussing. Vend, too, didn't seem to know if he was on his head or his heels. It was this that startled us so: "What can have become of them all?"

I heard no more. I really believe I swooned, but at the next station we saw consternation on every face. I pinched myself to see if I was dreaming. I tried to persuade myself I was. A passenger got in; he did not look quite as dazed as some did, but savage and cross. For a time no one spoke; at last someone said aloud, "What on earth's become of them?" and the cross-looking man, who got in last, growled out, "That's the worst of it; they are not *on earth*; they are gone. My boy always said it would be so. From the very first moment I heard it, I knew what had happened; often he has warned me. I still have his voice ringing in my ears.

" 'I tell you, in that night there will be two men in one bed: the one will be taken, and the other will be left' (Luke 17:34).

"I know only too well 'that night' was *last* night. It makes me so savage I don't know what to do."

Now, I was an atheist and did not believe the Bible. For the last thirty years I had stuck to my opinions, and when I heard men talk religious trash, I invariably objected.

But this seemed altogether different. I tell you, for a thousand pounds I couldn't have said a word. I just hoped it would all turn out a dream, but the farther we went, the more certain it became that we were all awake and that by some unaccountable visitation of Providence, a number of people had suddenly disappeared in the night.

The whole of society was unhinged; everybody had to do somebody else's work. Cabs were not scarce, but some of those who drove them seemed unlicensed and new to their work. The shutters in some of the shops were up, and on getting to my bank, I heard the keys had only just been found.

Everyone was silent and afraid lest some great misfortune was coming. I noticed we all seemed to mistrust one another, and yet as each fresh clerk, turned up late, entered the counting room, a low whisper went round. The chief cashier, as I expected, did not come.

Business was at a standstill. I hoped as the day wore on that it would revive, but it did not. The clerks went off without asking my permission, and I was left alone. I did not know what to do. I could not leave, or they might say the bank had stopped payment, and yet I felt I could not stay there. Business seemed to have lost its interest and money its value. I put up the shutters myself, and at once noticed that a change had come over the city while I had been at the bank. *Then* all were trying to fill the void places; *now* it seemed as if the attempt had failed.

In the city some of the streets had that dismal Sunday appearance, while a few houses had been broken into; but in the main thoroughfares there was a dense mass of people, hurrying, it struck me, they knew not where. Some seemed dazed, others almost mad with terror. At the stations confusion reigned, and I heard there had been some terrible accidents. I went into my club, but the waiters had gone off without leave, and one had to help oneself.

As evening came on, I saw the lurid reflection of several fires, but, horrible to say, no one seemed to mind, and I felt myself that if the whole of London were burned, and I with it, I would not care. For the first time in my life I no longer feared death: I looked on it as a friend.

As the gas was not lit, and darkness came down upon us, one heard cries and groans. I tried to light the gas, but it was not turned on. I remembered there was a candle in the writing room. I went and lit it, but of course it did not last long. I groped my way into the dining room and helped myself to some wine, but I could not find much, and what I took seemed to have no effect; and when I heard voices, they fell on me as if I were in a dream. They were talking of the Bible, though, and it now seemed the one book worth thinking of, yet in our vast club library I doubt if I would have found a single copy.

One said: "What haunts me are the words 'Watch therefore.' You can't *watch* now."

I thought of my dinner party. Little had I imagined a week ago, when I issued the invitations, how I would be passing the hour.

Suddenly I remembered the secretary
had been a religious fanatic, and I made
my way slowly to his room, knocking over
a table, in my passage, with glasses on it. It
fell with a crash that sounded through the
house, but no one noticed it. By the aid of
a match, I saw candles on his writing table
and lit them. Yes! As I thought, there was his
Bible. It was open as if he had been reading
it when called away, and another book I had
never seen before lay alongside it—a sort of
index.

The Bible was open at Proverbs, and
these verses, being marked, caught my eye:

"Because I have called and you refused,
I have stretched out my hand and no
one regarded. . .I also will laugh at your
calamity; I will mock when your terror
comes" (Proverbs 1:24, 26).

I had never thought before of God
laughing—of God mocking. I had fancied
man alone did that. Man's laughing had
ended now—I saw that pretty plain.

I had a hazy recollection of a verse that
spoke of men wanting the rocks to fall on
them, so I looked it up in the index. Yes,
there was the word "Rock," and some of the
passages were marked with a pencil. One
was Deuteronomy 32:15: "He forsook God
who made him, and scornfully esteemed the

Rock of his salvation."

Perhaps he marked that passage after he had had a talk with me. How well I remember the earnestness with which he pressed salvation upon me that day and assured me that if I only yielded myself to the Lord I would understand the peace and joy he talked about. But it was no use. I remember I only scoffed at him and said mockingly that his God was a myth, and time would prove it, and he answered, "Never. 'Heaven and earth will pass away, but My words will by no means pass away.' He may come tonight."

I laughed and said, "What odds will you take? I lay you long ones."

Another passage marked was 1 Samuel 2:2, "Nor is there any rock like our God," and lower still "Man who built his house on the rock."

I had no need to look that one up. I knew what it referred to, and then my eye caught Matthew 27:51, "The earth quaked, and the rocks were split." That was when Christ died to save sinners, died to save me—and yet I had striven against Him all my life. I could not bear to read more. I shut the book and got up. There were some texts hanging over the fireplace:

"Repent therefore and be converted,

that your sins may be blotted out" (Acts 3:19).

"The blood of Jesus Christ His Son cleanses us from all sin" (1 John 1:7).

"Now is the accepted time; behold, now is the day of salvation" (2 Corinthians 6:2).

As I turned to leave the room, these caught my eye, and I said, "Well, I have been a fool."

Tom looked up from the little booklet, a look of bewilderment in his eyes.

"The likelihood of the whole story is little less than startling," he murmured. His eyes dropped down to the book again, and he read the last line aloud: " 'Well, I have been a fool.' "

Reflectively, he added: "And I am as big a fool as the man in that book!"

He reverently laid the book down on the table by his bedside and switched off the light. "Of course, I know *historically* all the events of the Christ's life. His death, His resurrection, and—and—well, *there*, I think, my knowledge ends. In a vague way I have always known that the Bible said something of a great final solution to all the world drama—an award time of some kind, a millennium of perfect, well, perfect everything that is peaceful and— Oh, I don't know much about it now, after all. I am very much in a fog."

For a moment or two he tried to disentangle his many thoughts; then, with a weary little sigh, he gave up the task, murmuring, "*I* certainly am not ready for any such event. If there is to be a hideous leaving behind of the unready, then I should be left to all that unknown hideousness."

Myriad thoughts crowded upon his brain. Finally he gave up trying to think out the problem, telling himself that with the coming of the new day he would begin a definite search for the real facts of this great mystery—the Second Coming of Christ.

By an exercise of his will, he finally settled himself to sleep.

Chapter 12

❧

The Center of the Earth

"Will you come into my workroom, Mr. Hammond? It is a kind of sanctum to me as well as a workroom, and I always feel that I can talk freer there than anywhere else."

It was the Jew, Abraham Cohen, who said these words. His visitor was Tom Hammond. It was the morning after Tom had been troubled about *Long Odds* and its mysterious subject.

Jew and Gentile had had a few moments' general talk in the sitting room downstairs, but Cohen wanted to see his visitor alone—to be where nothing could interrupt their conversation.

Tom's first vision of Cohen's workroom amazed him. The apartment was a large one and, besides being a workroom, had the character of a study, den, sanctum—anything of that order that best pleases the reader.

But it was the finished work that chiefly arrested the attention of Tom, and in wondering tones he cried, "It is all so exquisitely fashioned! But *what* can it be for?"

Cohen searched his visitor's face with his deep, grave eyes.

"Will you give me your word, Mr. Hammond," he asked, "that you will hold in strict confidence the fact that this work is here in this place, if I tell you what it is for?"

"I do give you my word of honor, Mr. Cohen." As he spoke, Tom held forth his hand. The Jew grasped his hand, then the Jew said, "I do not wish to bind you to any secrecy as to the fact that such work as this is being performed in England, but only that you should preserve the secret of the whereabouts of the work and workers." With a sudden glow of pride he cried, "This work is for the New Temple!"

"The New Temple? I don't think I quite understand you, Mr. Cohen. Where is this temple being built?"

"It is not yet begun," replied the Jew. "That is, the actual rearing has not yet begun, though the preparations are well forward. The New Temple is to be at Jerusalem. There can be no other site for the temple of Jehovah save Zion, the city of our God— the center of the world."

Crossing the room to where a map of the world hung on the wall, the Jew took a ruler and, laying one end of it on Barrow Point, Alaska, he marked the spot on the ruler where it touched Jerusalem. From Jerusalem to Wrangel Land, Siberia, farther east, he showed by his ruler that he got practically the same measurement as when he did it from the west. From Jerusalem to North Cape, Scandinavia, and from Jerusalem to the Cape of Good Hope, he showed again that each was practically the same distance.

"Always, always is Zion the center of the inhabited earth!" he cried in quiet, excited tones. Moving quickly back to Tom's side, he said: "Did you ever think of this, sir, that practically speaking, all the nations west of Jerusalem—those of Europe—write from west to east—that is, toward the city of our God; while all the Asiatic races—those east of Zion—write from east to west—just the opposite—but always *toward* Zion? No, no, sir; there can be no other place on earth for the New Temple of Jehovah save Jerusalem. Read Ezekiel, from the fortieth chapter, sir, and you will see how glorious a temple Jehovah is to have soon. 'Show the house to the people of Israel,' God said in a vision to His prophet, 'and let them build it after the sum, the pattern which I show you.' And that, sir, is what we are doing."

"Who are the *we* who are doing this? Who makes the plans, gives the orders, finds the funds?"

"Wealthy, patriotic men of our people, sir. We as a race are learning that soon Messiah will come, and we are proving our belief by preparing for the House of our God. Italian Jews all over Italy are carving the richest marbles; wrought iron, wondrous works in metal, gold and silver ornaments, cornices, chapiters, bells for the high priest's robes, and a myriad of other things are being prepared, so that the moment the last restriction on our land is removed, we will begin to ship the several prepared parts to the temple of Palestine, as the Gentiles term our land."

A curious little smile flittered over his face as he added, "The very march of modern times in the East is all helping to make the consummation of our work easier. The new railways laid from the coast to Jerusalem are surely part of the providence of our God. When Messiah comes, sir, we shall be waiting ready for Him, I trust."

"But do you not know," Tom interrupted, "that according to every record of history as well as the New Testament, all Christendom has believed, for all the ages since, that the Messiah came nearly two thousand years ago?"

"The *Nazarene*?"

There was as much or more of pity than scorn in the voice of the Jew as he uttered the word.

"How could *He* be the Messiah, sir?" he went on. "Could any good thing come out of Nazareth? Besides, *our* Messiah is to redeem Israel, to deliver them from the hand of the oppressor and to gather again into one nation all our scattered race. No, no! The Nazarene could not be *our* Messiah!"

Turning quickly to Tom, he asked, "Are *you* a Christian, sir?"

For a moment Tom was startled by the suddenness

of the question. He found no immediate word of reply.

"You are a *Gentile*, of course, Mr. Hammond," the Jew went on, "but are you a Christian? For it is a curious fact that I find very few Gentiles whom I have met, even *professed* Christians, and fewer still who ever pretend to live up to their profession."

Tom recovered himself sufficiently to say, "Yes, I am a Gentile, of course, and I *suppose* I am—er—"

It struck him as extraordinary that he would find it difficult to state why he supposed he was a Christian.

While he hesitated the Jew went on: "Why should you say you *suppose*, sir? Is there nothing distinctive enough about the possession of Christianity to give assurance of it to its possessor? I do not *suppose* I am a *Jew*—by religion I mean, and not merely by race. No, sir, I do not suppose, for I *know* it. There is all the difference in the world, between the mere theology and the religion of the faith we profess. The religion is life, it seems to me; theology is only the science of that life."

Both men were so utterly absorbed in their talk that they did not hear a touch on the handle of the door. It was only as it opened that they turned round. Zillah stood framed in the doorway. Cohen, who saw her every day, realized that she had never looked so radiantly beautiful before. She had almost burst into the room but paused as she saw that a stranger was present.

"Excuse me," she began. "I had no idea you had a friend with you, Abraham."

She would have retreated, but he stopped her with an eager "Come in, Zillah."

She advanced, gazing in curious inquiry at Tom.

"This is Mr. Tom Hammond, editor of *The Courier*, Zillah," Cohen explained to the young girl. To Tom he added, "My wife's sister, Zillah Robart."

The introduced pair shook hands. The young Jew went on to explain to Zillah how the great editor came to be visiting him.

Tom's eyes were fixed upon the vision of loveliness that the Jewess made. He had seen female loveliness in many lands. He had gazed upon women who seemed too lovely for earth. But this Jewish maiden—she was beyond all his thought or knowledge of feminine loveliness.

While Cohen talked for a moment or two, and Zillah's eyes were fixed upon her brother-in-law, Tom's gaze was riveted upon the lovely girl.

He realized, in that first moment of full gazing upon her, how faded every other female face must ever seem beside her glorious beauty. With a strange freak of mental conjuring, Madge Finisterre and that interrupted tête-à-tête rose up before him, and a sudden sense of relief swept over him that George Carlyon had returned at the moment that he did.

"It is all so strange, so wonderful to me, what I have seen and heard here," he jerked out as Cohen finished his explanation.

Tom spoke to the beautiful girl, whose lustrous eyes had suddenly come back to his face.

For a moment or two longer, he voiced his admiration of the separate pieces of finished work and spoke of his own growing interest in the Jewish race.

The great black eyes that gazed upward into his grew liquid with the evident emotion that filled the soul of the beautiful girl. With the frank, hearty, simple gesture of the perfectly unconventional woman, she held forth her hand to Tom as she said, "It is so good of you, sir, to speak thus of my brother-in-law's work and of our race. There are few who speak kindly of us. Even though, as a nation, you English give our poor persecuted people sanctuary, yet there are few who care for us or speak kindly of us, and fewer still who speak kindly to us."

Tom warmly clasped the little hand that she offered him, almost forgetting himself as he gazed down into her expressive face and listened to her rich, musical voice.

The olive of the girl's cheeks warmed under the power of his gaze. He saw the warm color rise and remembered himself, shifted his eyes, and released her hand.

"I must not stay another moment, Abraham," she cried, turning to the Jew. "Adah would be vexed if I were late."

She turned back to Tom, but before she could speak, he was saying, "Good-bye, Miss Robart. I hope we may meet again. What your brother-in-law has already told me only incites me to come again and see him, for there are many things I want to know."

He shook hands with the girl again. His eyes met hers, and again he saw the olive cheeks suddenly warm.

Ten minutes later he was driving back to his office, his mind in a strange whirl, the beautiful face of Zillah Robart filling his vision.

He pulled himself up at last and laughed as he murmured, "And I am the man whose pulses had never been quickened by the sight or the touch of a woman until I met her—"

The memory of Madge Finisterre flashed into his mind. He smiled to himself as he mused, "Even when I seemed most smitten by Madge, I told myself I was not sure that love had anything to do with my feelings. Now I know it had not."

His eyes filled suddenly with a kind of staring wonder as he cried out in a low, startled undertone, "Am I inferring to myself that this sudden admiration for Zillah Robart has any element of love in it?"

He smiled at his own unuttered answer. The cab pulled up at the door of the office at that moment. He came back sharply to everyday things.

Chapter 13

❧

A Demon

Madge Finisterre awoke early on the morning after that discussion about herself concerning Tom's possible proposal.

With startling suddenness, as she lay still a moment, a vision of the pastor of Balhang came to her mind. Then a strange thing happened to her, for a yearning sense of homesickness suddenly filled her.

She tried to laugh at herself for her "childishness," as she called it, and sprang from her bed to prepare for her bath. Standing for one instant by the bedside, she murmured, "But, after all, it is time I was paddling across again. I must think this all out seriously. Anyway, I'll get my bath and dress and go for a stroll before breakfast."

Half an hour later she was dressed and ready for her expedition. As she passed the office on her way out, they were sorting the morning mail. She waited for her letter. There was only one, but it was from home.

Racing back to her room, she tore it open with an eagerness born, unconsciously to herself, of the nostalgia that had seized upon her three-quarters of an hour before.

There were two large, closely written sheets in the letter—one from her father and one from her mother. Each told their own news.

She read her father's first; every item interested her, though as she read she seemed to feel that there was all through it an underlying strain of longing for her return.

"Dear old Poppa!" she murmured.

Suddenly her eyes took in the two lines of postscript jammed close to the bottom edge of the first sheet. Her heart seemed to stand still as she read: "Pastor is considered sick. Doctor can't make his case out."

"Pastor sick!" She gasped the words aloud; then, turning swiftly to her mother's letter, she cried, "Momma will tell more than this!"

Her eyes raced over the written lines. Her mother said a little more than her father had said about the sickness of their friend and pastor; not much, though, in actual words, but to the disturbed heart of the young girl, there seemed to her much deeper meaning.

An excited trembling came upon her for a few moments. The next instant she got hold of herself, and folding the letters and replacing them in the envelope, she cried out quietly but sharply, "The boat from Southampton sails at two today. I'll catch that!"

The next instant she was taking off her hat and jacket and beginning to pack.

Now and then she talked to herself: "Sick, is he? Poor old Pastor! I guess I know what's the matter with him, and I'll put him right in five minutes."

She smiled as she went on: "I guess, too, I've found out what's the matter with me—I want to be a pastor's wife! I wonder how Uncle Archibald and George will take my sudden departure. Well, I'm glad George is out of town. It's best, perhaps, that I should leave without seeing him."

By eleven that forenoon she had left Waterloo. Her uncle had seen her off from the station. He wanted to accompany her to Southampton, but she would not hear of it.

"I want to be very quiet all the way down," she said, "and write some important letters. Make my excuses to everybody, and explain that I only had an hour or two to do everything."

At the last moment her uncle slipped an envelope into her hand, saying, "You are not to open it until you have been traveling a quarter of an hour."

Then came the good-byes, and—off.

She had been traveling *nearly* a quarter of an hour when she opened the envelope. There was a brief, hearty, loving note inside, in her uncle's handwriting, expressing the joy her visit had given him and his sense of loneliness at her going, and saying:

> *Please, dear Madge, accept the enclosed in*
> *second envelope as a souvenir of your visit,*
> *from your affectionate*
>
> > *Nunkums*

She opened the smaller envelope. To her breathless amazement, she found a Bank of England note for one thousand pounds. When she recovered herself a little, a smile filled her eyes as she murmured, "Fancy an American Methodist pastor's wife with a thousand pounds of her own!"

The train was rushing on; she remembered that she had a special letter to write. She opened her bag and took out writing materials. The carriage rocked tremendously, but she managed to pen her letter and then enclosed it in an envelope.

Tom had just settled himself down to work when a letter, bearing the Southampton postmark, was delivered to him. Opening it and reading "My dear Mr. Hammond," he turned next to the signature. "Madge Finisterre?" he cried softly under his breath. Wonderingly he turned back to the first page and read:

> *You will be surprised to know that when you*
> *receive this I shall be steaming down channel*
> *en route for New York. I got letters from home*
> *this morning that made it imperative that I*

should start at once.

I cannot leave without thanking you for all your kindness to me. It has been a pleasure to have known you, and I sincerely hope that we may meet again someday.

Now I am going to take you right into my confidence, Mr. Hammond, for who is so discreet as a "prophet"?

Yesterday evening, after dinner, I had a long talk alone with myself. I had had a very pleasant tête-à-tête tea with a friend—perhaps you may remember this—and while I went over in mind many things in connection with that tête-à-tête, especially the events immediately preceding the interruption, I suddenly realized a sense of longing for home.

A night or two before I sailed from America, our pastor asked me to be his wife. He was awfully in earnest, poor fellow; and I could see how love for me—gay, frivolous little me—was consuming him. I was startled at the proposition and told him frankly that I did not know my own mind, but that if ever I found out that I loved him, I would come right away and tell him so. I found out this morning, when I heard that he was dangerously sick, that I wanted him as much as ever he wanted me.

I am going back to my pastor to nurse him back to health. Please keep all this in absolute confidence, for I have not given even a hint of

> *it to my uncle. Whenever you visit the States,*
> *be sure to come and visit me, for no one will*
> *be more welcome from the Old Country than*
> *yourself.*
>
> *By the way, dear friend, with regard*
> *to your remark concerning the presence of a*
> *woman to make tea for you, keep the subject*
> *well before yourself, and when you see the lady*
> *who can really satisfy all your ideals, propose*
> *quickly, secure her, and do America by way of*
> *a honeymoon, and come and see me.*
>
>

Yours most sincerely,
Madge Finisterre
>

He smiled as he laid down the letter. For a moment all the bright, piquant personality of the writer filled his vision. Then, with a swiftness and completeness that was almost startling, her face vanished from his mind, and Zillah Robart, in all her radiant loveliness, took her place in his thoughts.

For a brief while he was absorbed in his new vision. The sudden entrance of Ralph Bastin dispelled his dreaming.

After a few moments' talk, Bastin cried, quite excitedly, "I say, Tom, those paragraphs of yours about the Jews are the talk of all London."

Without breaking the confidence reposed in him by Cohen, Tom told his friend what he had recently discovered as to the Jewish work on the materials for the New Temple.

"That's strange, Tom," returned Bastin. "I dropped in now as much as anything to tell you that last night I met Dolly Anstruther—you remember her, don't you?—the little Yorkshire girl that was learning sculpture when we were staying at Paris with Montmarte.

"She has just come back from Italy, where she has been three years. She told me how startled she was to hear from several sources about this New Temple business. She said she visited a very large studio in Milan and saw the most magnificent pillar she had ever seen. She asked the great artist what it was for, and he said, 'It is a pillar for the New Temple at Jerusalem.'

"In Rome she visited another great studio, and there she saw a duplicate of the Milan pillar and was told again, 'Oh, that is a pillar for the future temple at Jerusalem.' What does it all mean, Tom?"

"That is what I want to find out, Ralph. My intelligent Jew declares that the Messiah is coming. We, as Christians—nominal Christians, I mean, of course—same as you and I, Ralph, don't profess anything more—"

Bastin searched his friend's face with a sudden keenness but did not interrupt him by asking him what he meant.

"As nominal Christians," Tom went on, "we believe the Christ has already come. But the question has been around in my mind of late, does the Bible teach that Christ is coming again, and are all these strange movings among the Jews and in the politics of the world so many signs and—"

There came an interruption at that moment. They learned of the assassination of the Continental crowned head. Both men became journalists, pure and simple, in an instant.

Chapter 14

❧

Major Hadley on "The Coming!"

The next morning Tom was riding westward in the Tube. He sat back in the comfortable seat of the car, dipping into a book.

At that instant he heard someone mention the name of his paper. He glanced in the direction of the voices. Two gentlemen were talking together. It was evident that his own identity was utterly unknown to them.

"You're right, you're right," the second man was saying. "A very clever fellow, evidently, that editor of *The Courier.*"

"You have noticed, of course," the first man went on, "those striking paragraphs, of late, about the Jews. Though, to a keen student of the subject, they show a very superficial knowledge; still, it is refreshing to find a modern newspaper editor writing like that at all."

"Yes," the other said, "but it is strange how

few people, even Christian people, ever realize how intimately the future of the Jewish race is bound up with the truth of the coming of the Lord for His Church. I wish the editor of *The Courier*, and every other newspaper editor, could be induced to go this afternoon and hear Major Hadley speak on these things."

"British Museum!" called the conductor of the car. The two talkers got out. Tom also alighted. As he rode in the elevator to the street, he decided that he would hear this major on the subject that was occupying his own thoughts so much.

Three o'clock that afternoon found him one of a congregation of three to four hundred persons. He was amazed at the quality of the audience. He recognized a dozen well-known London clergymen and ministers, with a score of other equally well-known laymen—literary men, merchants, etc. All were of a superior class. There was a large sprinkling of ladies as well.

There was a subdued hum of whispering voices in the place. The hum suddenly ceased. Tom glanced quickly toward the platform. Half a dozen gentlemen and one or two ladies were taking their seats there. They bowed their heads in silent prayer.

A minute later a tall, fine-looking man rose to his feet and advanced to the rail. He held a hymnbook in his hand. His keen eyes swept the faces of the gathered people. Then in a clear, ringing voice like the voice of a military officer on the battlefield, he cried:

"Number three-twenty-four. Let every voice ring out in song."

Hammond opened the linen-covered book that had been handed to him.

The major gave out the first verse:

> *"It may be at morn, when the day is*
> *awaking,*
> *When sunlight thro' darkness and shadow*
> *is breaking,*
> *That Jesus will come in the fullness of*
> *glory,*
> *To take out of the world 'His own.'"*

> *"O Lord Jesus, how long?*
> *How long ere we shout the glad song*
> *Christ returneth! Hallelujah!*
> *Hallelujah! Amen!"*

A hundred thoughts and conflicting emotions filled him as he realized that these people were really inspired by the glorious hope of the return of the Christ. Once he shuddered as the thought presented itself to his mind, *How would* I *fare if this Christ came suddenly—came now?*

With the last sung note the voice of the major rang out again:

"General Sir R. P. Jones will lead us in prayer."

The prayer concluded, not a moment was wasted. In his clear, ringing tones, the major began: "Turn with me, if you will, dear friends, to the first chapter of the Acts of the Apostles, and the eleventh verse."

Tom wished that he had a Bible with him. It seemed to him that he was the only person there without one.

The major, pocket Bible in hand, continued: "Allow me, friends, to change one word in my reading, that the truth may come home clearer to our hearts. 'Men of London. . . This same Jesus, who was taken up from you into heaven, will so come in like manner as you saw Him go into heaven.' The second coming of our Lord and Savior Jesus Christ is, I believe, the central truth of real, true Christianity at this moment, and it should be carefully, diligently studied by every converted soul. It should be comprehended as far as scripture reveals it, and so apprehended that we should live in daily, hourly expectancy of that return.

"Many of you who are present this afternoon are not only conversant with this glorious matter but are living in the glad expectancy of the return of your Lord. But there are sure to be some here today to whom the whole subject is foreign, and to you I shall speak as frankly and simply as though we were having a chat."

Chapter 15

~

The Address

"Now to begin. Even in the Church of God there are whole multitudes to whom the very title of this afternoon's address is but jargon. They will not search the Word for it; they will barely tolerate its mention. Why? 'Oh,' say some, 'hidden things are not to be searched into.' Others there are who spiritualize every reference to the Lord's Second Coming and say, 'Yes, of course. He has come into my heart, or how else could I have become a child of God?'

"To these last, we would respectfully say, 'A coming into the air for His people, to take them up, is a totally different thing than coming into the heart to indwell as Savior and Keeper while we are traveling life's pathway.'

"Two distinct advents are plainly taught in scripture. The first, of Jesus' birth as a babe in Bethlehem, the second as 'Son of Man'—glorified, who will come in the clouds. Now, every Christian will admit that every scripture relating to the first advent, as to time, place, circumstances, was literally fulfilled. Then, with the same covenant scriptures in our hands, why should we not expect to see the predictions relating to the second advent also fulfilled to the very letter?

"We have our Lord's own definite promise in John fourteen: 'If I go. . .I will come again and receive you to Myself.' We are all agreed that He went. Well, in the same breath He said, 'I will come again.' Can any English be plainer? That promise cannot allude to conversion, and it certainly cannot allude to death, for death is a going to Him—if we are saved.

"This expectancy of Christ's return for His people was the only hope of the early Church; and over and over again in the Epistles it is shown to be the only hope of the Church, until that Church is taken out of the world. There never has been any comfort to bereaved ones in the thought of death, nor to any one of us who are living is there any comfort in the contemplation of death, except, of course, the thought of relief from weariness and suffering and in being translated to a painless sphere to be with Christ. But in the contemplation of the coming of Christ, there is the certainty of the gladdest meeting.

"There are two points I would emphasize here. First, that we must not confuse the second coming of our Lord with the end of the world. The uninstructed, inexperienced child of God feels a quaking of heart at all talk of such a coming.

"Such people shrink for the suddenness of it. They say that there is no preparatory sign to warn us of that coming. But that is not true.

"The Word of God gives many instructions as to the signs of Christ's near return, and the hour we live in shows us these signs on every hand, so that it is only those who are ignorant of the Word of God, or those who are carelessly or willfully blind to the signs around, who fail to see how near must be the moment of our Lord's return.

"The first sign of this return is an awakening of national life among the Jews that will immediately precede their return to their own land. Please turn with me to Matthew twenty-four. You who know your Bible will readily recall the subject matter of the previous chapter, and how our Lord after His terrible prediction upon Jerusalem added, 'See! Your house is left to you desolate; for I say to you, you shall see Me no more till you say, "Blessed is He who comes in the name of the Lord!" '

"This is Jewish, of course, but the whole matter of the future of the Jews and of the return of the Lord for His Church, and later on, with His Church, are bound up together. Presently, after uttering His last prediction, the disciples came to Him privately, saying, 'Tell us, when will these things be? And what will be the sign of Your coming, and of the end of the age?'

"Keep your Bibles open where you now have

them, friends, and note this—that the twofold answer of our Lord's is in the reverse order to the disciple's question. In verses four and five He points out what should not be the sign of His coming, while in verse six, He shows what should not be the sign of the end of the world. With these distinctions I will have more to say another day.

"This afternoon I want to keep close to the signs of the coming of the Lord. Read then the thirty-second and thirty-third verses: 'Now learn this parable from the fig tree: When its branch has already become tender and puts forth leaves, you know that summer is near. So you also, when you see all these things, know that'—look in the margins of your Bible, please, and note that the 'it' of the text becomes 'He,' which is certainly the only wise translation—'when you see all these things, know that He is near—at the doors!'

"Now, I hardly need remind the bulk of you gathered here this afternoon that the fig tree, in the Gospels, represents Israel. Now, with this key of interpretation before us, how pointed becomes this first sign of the return of our Lord. When, He says, the fig tree 'puts forth' her leaves—when the Jewish nation shows signs of a revival of national life and vitality—then know that the coming of the Lord draws near.

"The careful reader of the daily press ought to have long ago been awakened to the fact that, after thousands of years, the national life of Israel is awakening. The Jew is returning to his own land—Palestine.

"Only a year or two ago, the world was electrified by hearing of the formation of that wonderful Zionist movement. How it has spread and grown! There are now nearly three times the number of Jews in and around Jerusalem than there were after the return from the Babylonish captivity. Agricultural settlements are extending all over the land. Vineyards and olive grounds are springing up everywhere.

"Now note a remarkable fulfillment of prophecy. Turn to Isaiah seventeen, verses ten and eleven: 'Therefore you will plant pleasant plants and set out foreign seedlings; in the day you will make your plant to grow, and in the morning you will make your seed to flourish; but the harvest will be a heap of ruins in the day of grief and desperate sorrow.'

"In the early months of 1894, the Jews ordered two million vine slips from America, which they planted in Palestine. There is the fulfillment of the first part of that prophecy, and if we are justified in believing, as we think we are, that the return of the Lord is imminent, then, as the tribulation will doubtless immediately follow that return, and the taking out of the Church from the world, then the great gathering in of the harvest of those vines will be in 'the day of grief and desperate sorrow.'

"Now, let me read to you, friends, an extract from the testimony of an expert, long resident in Palestine:

" 'There is not the shadow of a doubt,' he writes, 'as to the entire changing of the climate of the land here. The former and latter rains are becoming the regular order of the seasons, and this is doubtless due to the fact that the new colonists are planting trees everywhere where they settle. The land, for thousands of years, has been denuded of trees, so that there was nothing to attract the clouds, etc.

" 'Comparing the rainfall for the last five years, I find that there has been about as much rain in April as in March; whereas, comparing five earlier years, from 1880 through 1885, I find that the rainfall in April was considerably less than in March, and if we go back further still, we find that rain in April was almost unknown.

" 'Thus God is preparing the land for the people. The people, too, are being prepared for the land. The day is fast approaching when the Lord 'will arise and have mercy on Zion.'

"I hardly need to tell you what even the secular press has been giving some most striking articles about quite recently—namely, the quiet preparation on the part of the Jews of everything for the rebuilding of the temple at Jerusalem.

"I see, by the lighting up of your faces, that you are familiar with the fact that gates, pillars, marbles, ornaments, and all else requisite for the immediate building of the New Temple are practically complete and only await the evacuation of the Mohammedan, with all his abominations, from Jerusalem, to be hurried to the site of the old temple, and to be reared, a new temple to Jehovah, by the Jew. Any day, Turkey, in desperate straits for money, may sell Palestine to the Jews.

"The Jews are to return to their land in unbelief of Christ being the Messiah. They will build their temple, reorganize the old elaborate services, the lamb will be slain again, and—but all else of this time belongs to another address. What we have to see this afternoon is that the fig tree—the Jewish nation—is building, and to hear Jesus Christ saying to us, 'When you see all these things, know that He is near—at the doors!'

"Another sign of the return of our Lord is to be the worldwide preaching of the Gospel. Now, in this connection, let me give a word of correction of a common error on this point.

"The Bible nowhere gives a hint that the world is to be converted before the return of the Lord for His Church. As a matter of fact, the world—the times— are to grow worse and worse; more polished, more cultured, cleverer, better educated, yet grosser in soul, falser in worship. The bulk of the Church shall have the form of godliness but deny the power.

"Men shall be lovers of themselves, covetous, unfaithful, lovers of pleasure. I need not enlarge further on this side of the subject, except to repeat that the Word of God is most plain and emphatic on this point, that the return of our Lord is to be marked by a fearful turning aside from vital godliness. But with all this, there is to be a worldwide proclamation of the truth of salvation in Jesus. Not necessarily that every individual soul shall hear it but that all nations will have it preached to them.

"Now, in this connection, let me mention a fact that has deeply impressed me. It is this: that the greatest reawakening in the hearts of individual Christians in all the churches as testified to by all concerned, agrees, in time, with the awakening of the Church of Christ to the special need of intercession for foreign missions—namely, from 1863 through 1875.

"I must close for this afternoon. I pray you all to be much in prayer for blessing on the attempt to open up these wondrous truths.

"Do any of you know any editors of a daily paper? If so, write to them, draw attention to these expositions, urge your editors to come. Oh, if only we could capture the daily press! What an extended pulpit, what a far-reaching voice would our subject immediately possess!

"I don't quite know how far I ought to go on this line, but even as I speak, it comes to me to ask you if anyone here present is acquainted with the evidently gifted, open-minded editor of *The Courier*. We have all, of course, been struck by his own utterances in his 'From the Prophet's Chamber' column. Oh, that he could be captured for Christ; then his paper would doubtless be a clarion for his Lord!"

Tom turned hot and cold. He trusted that no one had recognized him. He would be glad to get away unrecognized. Yet he was not offended by the speaker's personal allusion to him. He felt that the major's soul rang true.

"So, I say," the major continued, " 'The coming of the Lord draws near.' May God help us to quicken all our hearts and purify our lives, that we may not be ashamed at His coming.

"And to any who are here who are not converted, may God help you to seek His face, that you may not be 'left' when He shall suddenly, silently snatch away His Church out of the godless generation.

"Think of what that will mean, unsaved friend, if you are here today. Left! Left behind! When the Spirit of God will have been taken out of the earth. When Satan will dwell on the earth—for with the coming of Christ into the air, Satan, 'the prince of the power of the air,' will have to descend.

"Christ and Satan can never live in the same realm. O God, save anyone here from being left behind, to come upon the unspeakable judgments that will follow the taking out of the world of the Church!

"It is high time for us all to awaken. God keep us awake and watching for our Lord, for His precious name's sake. Our time has gone, friends."

As Tom left the hall, the major's words rang in his heart and mind. They forced themselves upon his brain and clamored to be listened to.

Chapter 16

❧

Her Cabin Companion

"There'll be one other lady with you in your cabin, miss."

The berth steward's announcement in no way disconcerted Madge Finisterre. She had had two cabin companions on the outward voyage.

She was arranging her cabin necessaries when her fellow traveler entered. She was a small, winsome girl, with a yearning sweetness in her gray eyes. With half a dozen words of exchanged greeting and a very warm handshake, the pair became instant friends.

As the vessel forged her way down channel that evening, a glorious moon shining down upon them, the two girls, arm in arm, paced the promenade deck talking. The subject of the acute distress among the poor and unemployed in all the world's great cities came up between them.

"Oh, if only our Lord would come quickly!" cried

the girl—Katie Harland was her name.

"What do you mean, Katie?" Madge's voice was full of wonder.

"I mean that—"

The fragile girl paused; then, glancing quickly up into Madge's face, she cried, "You love Jesus, of course, Madge? You are saved, dear, and looking for His coming?"

For an instant Madge was silent. Then, with a deep sigh, she replied, "Oh, me! I am afraid I am not saved, as you call it. Katie, dear, the fact is—"

She halted in her speech. She did not know how to put into words all that her friend's question had aroused within her.

While she halted thus, the girl at her side put her arms about her, clasping her with an "I will not let you go" kind of clasp, as she cried softly, "Oh, my darling, you must not lie down tonight until you know you are Christ's. Then—after that, nothing can ever matter. No matter what comes, all is well!"

It was past midnight before the two girls climbed into their berths, but by that time Madge knew that she had passed from death into life.

Before the vessel reached New York, she had learned something of the truth of the coming return of the Lord.

On the quay, when they landed, the two girls bade each other a sorrowful farewell.

"We will meet in heaven, Katie, if not again on

earth," sobbed Madge.

"In the air, my darling," replied the other. "Let's not lose sight of that."

Katie Harland's friends, who had traveled to meet her from Denver, carried her off, and Madge took the car to the Central.

One hour later she boarded the train and began the last lap of her long journey.

Her spirits rose higher every moment. She had conceived a very bold idea, and she was going to carry it through after her own fashion. She sent no message of warning of her coming, as this would spoil her little plot.

Her eyes rested with delight on every place she passed. At Duchess Junction she had to change trains. To her joy, she met no one from Balhang; there was not a soul at the depot whom she even knew by sight.

Just before her train reached Balhang, she donned a thick brown gauze veil. No one could see her face through it to recognize her. There would be nothing to detain her at the depot, for her baggage was to be sent by express to her home.

The train stopped; she alighted. Several people peered hard at her, the depot manager especially as he took her check, but no one recognized her. She passed on. Twenty yards from the depot, she met Judge Anstey.

She stopped him with a "Good day, Judge; can I speak with you?"

"Certainly, madam," the official replied genially.

"Come aside, Judge," she whispered. "I don't want anyone to recognize me or to hear what I am saying to you, should people pass."

As he moved on by her side in the direction she wished, she whispered, "I have put on this thick veil, Judge, so as not to be recognized. I am Madge Finisterre."

"You don't say!" he gasped. "I knew the voice but could not recall whose it was. I hadn't heard a breath of your coming home, Miss Madge."

"I let no one, not even Momma and Poppa, know that I was coming," she replied. "The fact is, Judge—"

She was glad, as she prepared to take him into her confidence, that the thick veil would hide the hot color that she felt leap into her face.

"Momma wrote me," she went on, "that the pastor was very sick and that the doctor didn't understand his case. I only got the letter last Saturday morning. The boat was to start that day at two, but I caught it, for I knew that would cure the pastor."

She felt how fiercely the blushes burned in her cheeks, but assured that he could not see them, she went on:

"Just before I started for Europe, Judge, Pastor told me he loved me and asked me to be his wife—"

She watched the amused amazement leap into the judge's face and smiled at his low whistle.

"I told him," she continued, "I could make him no definite promise, as I was not quite sure of myself, but that when I was, I would not wait for him to ask me again—I would come and tell him. I am going straight to him now, Judge, and I want you to give me a clear quarter of an hour's start. While I am gone to fix him up and to make him happy, I want you to go 'long to Momma and Poppa, and bring them right along with you, and marry me and Pastor as soon as you git up to us. So long for a quarter of an hour."

Without another word she moved swiftly away.

❧

The French windows of the pastor's sitting room were open, for the day was like a spring one. Madge moved quickly across the patch of grass, mounted the stoop, and peered in.

In a large rocker, looking very frail and ill, the young pastor was lying back with his eyes closed.

Madge felt her eyes fill with tears. She lifted the disguising veil and wiped the salt drops away. She did not lower her veil again, but with a little glad cry of "Homer, dear love!" she crossed the threshold and dropped to her knees by his side, flung her arms around his neck, and laid her hot lips to his.

It was like a dream to him—a wonderful, delicious dream. His thin arms clasped her. His kisses were rained upon her, but at first he found no words to say. Between their passionately exchanged kisses, she poured out, in rapid speech, how she came to be there.

"I have not seen Momma or Poppa yet," she explained, "but I met Judge Anstey down by the depot. I have sent him home for Momma and Poppa; they will be here in no time now. The judge will come with them and will marry us right off, dear. For you do want some nursing."

He found his voice at last, declared that her coming, her first kiss, had made him strong, that he would need no nursing now that she had come. Getting to his feet, he gathered her into his arms and rained fresh kisses upon her lips, her cheeks, her brow, her eyes.

She managed to whisper the good news: "I have found Jesus, dear, or He found me, and now—"

A sound of voices and of hurrying steps outside checked her. She had only time to tear herself from his arms when her mother and father reached her side.

An hour later, when the judge had been and gone again, Madge Finisterre was the wife of the pastor.

Chapter 17

❧

Casting a Shoe

It was two hours after midnight when Tom was free at last. But he did not go to bed. His soul was disturbed. What he had heard at the major's meeting had stirred a myriad of disquieting thoughts within him, and now that he was clear to do it, he shut himself up alone with a Bible and began to go over every point of the major's address. He had taken abundant notes in shorthand, paying special attention to the texts quoted and referred to.

At the end of an hour, he looked up from his Bible. There was a wondering amazement in his eyes, a strange, perplexed knitting of his brows.

"It is all most marvelous!" he murmured. "There is not a flaw or hitch anywhere in the major's statements or reasoning. The scriptures prove, to the hilt, every word that he uttered."

He smiled to himself as he said aloud, "I would not sleep if I went to bed; I will go out."

Ten minutes after leaving his chambers, he was inside the park he loved best. Everything was eerily still and silent. The air was as balmy as a morning in May or September.

He moved slowly, thoughtfully, through paths as familiar to him as the rooms he occupied at home.

"And the Christ might come today!" he mused. "As Major Hadley showed plainly from the Bible, there is no other prophetic event to transpire before His coming."

Almost unconsciously he paused in his walking. "If He came today, came now, what about me? Where would I come in?"

He realized the fact that, according to the major, he was quite unprepared for Christ's coming, because he was still unsaved. He shivered slightly.

The stars faded out of sight. The cold gray light of dawning day moved into the eastern horizon. He turned to face the spot where he knew the great clock tower of Westminster could be seen. A light burned high aloft in the tower, telling that England's legislators were still in session.

Slowly, thoughtfully, he turned back to walk home.

"If Christ came at this instant," he mused, "how many of those legislators would be ready to meet Him? And what of the teeming millions of this mighty city? God help us all! What blind fools we are!"

In spite of his night vigil, Tom was in the office at his usual hour. He had been there about an hour when there came a short, sharp rap on the door. In response to his "Come in!" Joyce, the drunken reporter, lurched in. Somehow he had contrived to elude those on duty in the inquiry office.

He was the worse for drink, and in response to Hammond's sharp queries: "What do you want? How came you here unannounced?" he began to "beg the loan of five shillings."

"Not a copper!" cried Tom.

Joyce whined for it.

Tom refused more sharply.

The drunken wretch cringed and whimpered for "just 'arf a crown." The fellow began to bluster then to threaten.

"If you don't leave this room, I'll hurl you out," cried Tom, "and put you in custody of the police."

The drunk straightened his limp form as well as he was able as he hiccuped: "All rightsh, Tom Ham'n'd. Every dawg hash hish day. You're havin' yoursh now, all rightsh—all rightsh—but I'll—*hic*—do fur yer; I'll—*hic*—ruin yer; I'll—"

Tom darted from his place by the table. The next instant he would have put his threat of "hurling out" into effect, but the drunken braggart did not wait for him, for he shuffled out of the room, cursing hideously.

As the door closed on him, Tom muttered, "I'll see Ralph then go out for a couple of hours. I'll go and see Cohen."

It was interesting how often he found excuses

to visit the Jew.

A quarter of an hour later, he drove up to the house of Cohen. He found him and his wife and Zillah on the point of starting for their synagogue.

"Will you go with us, Mr. Hammond?" Cohen asked.

Tom's eyes met Zillah's. Then he promptly said, "Yes."

"Right, then!" Cohen said, and the quartet left the house.

He had no opportunity of talking with Zillah, but he found his heart beating with a strange wildness whenever his eyes met hers—and they frequently met.

At the door of the synagogue, the party had to separate, the two women going one way, Cohen and Hammond another. The building was filling very fast. Presently it was packed to suffocation.

It was Tom's first sight of a Jewish congregation in a synagogue. It amazed him. The hatted men and bewigged women—these latter sat behind a grille. The gorgeousness of much of the female finery. The intriguing "praying shawls"—the "talith" of the men.

When the service was concluded, the building emptied. As they were walking homeward, Cohen's wife stopped to speak to some friends. The young Jew joined her. Tom found himself moving forward by Zillah's side.

"What an extraordinary service that was, Miss Robart!" he said.

"It was!" She glanced almost shyly away from

him, for unknown to himself, his eyes were full of the warmest admiration. She was conscious that his gaze was fixed on her. She was equally conscious that she was blushing furiously.

Perhaps it was to give her a chance to recover herself that his next question was on quite a different topic.

"Are you, Miss Robart," he said, "wholly wedded to the Jewish faith? Do you believe, for instance, that Jesus, the Nazarene, was an imposter?"

He heard the catch that came into her throat. Then, with a half-frightened look around, she lifted her eyes to his as she said, "I can trust you, Mr. Hammond, I know. You will keep my confidence, if I give it to you?"

His eyes answered her, and she went on.

"I have not dared to breathe a word of it to anyone, not even to my good brother-in-law, Abraham, but I am learning to love the Christ. I see how the prophecies of our forefathers—Isaiah especially—were all literally fulfilled in the life and work of Jesus of Nazareth. I see, too, that when next He comes, it will not be as our race supposes, as the Messiah to the Jews, but He will come in the air, and—"

She glanced sharply round. Some instinct told her her friends were coming.

"No more now," she whispered. "I will tell you more another time. I will myself know more tonight. I go twice a week to a mission room at Spitalfields—"

"What time?" he asked eagerly.

"Seven," she replied.

"Where is the place?" he went on.

She had just time to tell him. When Cohen and his wife came up, husband and wife began talking together. Zillah appeared to listen, but in reality she heard nothing of what they were saying, for a strange thing had happened.

She had dropped her hand by her side as the Cohens had rejoined them and had suddenly found her fingers clasped in Tom's hand.

What did it mean? she wondered. They had met often of late. She had read an unmistakable ardency in his eyes very often, when her glance met his. And deep in her own heart, she knew that all the woman love she would ever have to give a man she had unconsciously given to him. Was this sudden secret handclasp of his a silent expression of love on his part, or was it meant merely as an assurance of sympathy in the matter of her new faith?

She could not be sure which it was, but she let her plump fingers give a little pressure of response. How did he translate this response? she wondered. She had no way of deciding, except that her heart leaped wildly in a tumultuous delight as she felt how he gripped her fingers in a closer, warmer clasp.

They had reached the house by this time. Tom would not go in. He shook hands in parting with each, but his hold on Zillah's hand was longer than the others. He pressed the fingers meaningfully, and his eyes held an ardency that sent her heart into a new tumult.

As she passed into the house, she whispered to herself, "Will he be at Spitalfields tonight?"

Chapter 18

❧

TOLD IN A CAB

A quarter of an hour before the time Zillah had given him, Tom was waiting near the "Mission Hall for Jews," where the meeting was to be held. He was anxious that she not know of his proximity, so he kept out of sight.

Soon he saw her coming, and the light of a glad admiration leaped into his eyes. From behind a stall he watched her cross over to the door of the hall. Here she paused a moment and glanced around.

"I believe she half expected to see me somewhere near!" he murmured to himself.

She entered the hall. By the time her head was bowed in prayer, he had entered and had taken a seat on the last bench, the fourth behind hers. When she first raised her head from her silent prayer, she looked behind her. In her heart she was hoping he would be there. If he had not been bending in prayer, she might have seen him. After that she turned no more; the service soon occupied all her thoughts.

He, too, became utterly absorbed by the service, of which the address was the chief feature. It was largely expository, and from the first utterances of the speaker, it riveted Tom's attention.

The speaker, himself a converted Jew, took as his text Deuteronomy 21:22–23.

" 'If a man has committed a sin deserving of death, and he is put to death, and you hang him on a tree, his body shall not remain overnight on the tree, but you shall surely bury him that day, so that you do not defile the land which the Lord your God is giving you as an inheritance; for he who is hanged is accursed of God.' "

"Now, brothers, as far as I have been able to discover, in all the Hebrew records I have been able to consult, and in all the histories of our race, I have not found a single reference to a Hebrew official hanging of a criminal on a tree. To what, then, does this verse refer, and why is it placed in Jehovah's statute book? Now let us see if the New Testament will shed any light upon this."

Rapidly turning the pages of his Bible, he went on: "There is a book in the Christian scriptures known as the Epistle to the Galatians, which, in the tenth verse of the third chapter, repeats our own word from Deuteronomy: 'Cursed is everyone who does not continue in all things which are written in the book of the law, to do them,' and in the thirteenth verse says, 'Christ has redeemed us from the curse of the law, having become a curse for us (for it is written, "Cursed is everyone who hangs on a tree").'

"We all, as the sons of Abraham, believe that our father David's psalm beginning, 'My God, My God, why have You forsaken Me?' was never written out of his own experience but was prophetic of some other Person. Now, let me quote you some of the words of that psalm."

In clear, succinct language, the speaker, quoting verse after verse of the psalm, showed how literally the descriptions fitted into a death by crucifixion. Referring to the Gospel narratives of the death on the cross, he showed how they also fitted in with the description of Christ's death and how Christ actually took upon His dying lips the cry of the psalm, "My God, My God, why have You forsaken Me?"

Then with wonderful clarity he referred to parts of Isaiah 53 and showed that it was evident that only one particular type of death could have atoned for the sin of the human race, a death that would render the dying one accursed of the Almighty. The only death that would fully carry out that condition was crucifixion.

"Our race waited for the Messiah," he cried, "and He came. Our prophet Micah said, 'But you, Bethlehem Ephrathah, though you are little among the thousands of Judah, yet out of you shall come forth to Me the One to be Ruler in Israel.'

"The Christ was born at the only time in the

world's history when He could have been executed on a tree—crucified. At a time when the Roman—crucifixion was a Roman punishment—swayed our beloved land of Jewry. So that Paul, the great Jew, chosen of God to be apostle to the Gentiles, wrote after the crucifixion of Jesus, the Nazarene, 'According to the time, Christ died.'

"We must know the meaning of sin before we can understand the mystery of a crucified Christ. A beheaded, a stoned Christ could not have atoned for a guilty world, but only a God-cursed death, a tree-cursed death could have done this.

"And Christ was cursed for us—He who knew no curse of His own. Ah! Beloved, the guilt of the human race is the key to the cross.

"Times change, customs change, but sin remains, sin is ever the same, and only a living, personal trust in the crucified Christ can ever deliver the unsaved sinner from the wrath of God that abides on him."

The address closed. Tom awoke from his intense absorption of soul. He had long since utterly forgotten Zillah. He had only seen himself: at first, his own sin, and that his sin had nailed Christ to the cross. Then, better still, he saw the Christ.

Tom's soul received the great Revelation. He heard no word of the closing hymn and prayer but passed out into the open air a new man in Christ.

The mission leader had given an invitation to any who would like to be helped in soul matters to remain behind. Tom noticed that Zillah lingered.

It was half an hour before she came out. Tom had lived a lifetime of wonder in those thirty minutes.

Like one in a delicious dream, Zillah walked on a few yards. Suddenly she became aware of Tom's presence at her side.

"Zillah!"

He gave her no other word of greeting. It was the first time he had ever called the young girl by her first name. He took her hand and drew it through his arm. She barely noticed the tender action, for her soul was rioting in a newfound joy, and she poured out, in a few sentences, all the story of her supreme trust in Christ the Nazarene.

His voice was hoarse with many emotions as he said, "I, too, Zillah, have tonight seen Jesus Christ dying for my sin and have taken Him for my own personal Savior!"

Suddenly she realized how closely he was holding her to his side, how tight was the clasp of his hand upon hers. She looked up into his face to express her joy at his newfound faith. Their eyes met. A new meaning flashed in their exchanged glances.

"Let us take a cab, Zillah. I have something to say to you that I must say tonight."

Before she realized it, she was seated by his side in a cab.

There is a moment in every woman's life when her heart warns her of the coming of the great event in that life, when love is to be offered to her by the only man who has ever loomed large enough in her consciousness to be able to affect her existence.

This moment had suddenly, unexpectedly come to Zillah Robart.

Her heart warned her that the crisis was upon her. She had done nothing to precipitate it. It had met her, drawn her aside, and shut her up in the semidarkness of this vehicle with the only man she could ever love.

He had secured her hand; he held it in his strong, hot clasp. She held her breath in a strange, expectant ecstasy. Then the inevitable came. She felt its coming.

Tom was drawing her closer to himself. She was yielding to that drawing. She caught her breath again, and as she did so a rush of strange tears filled her eyes.

"Zillah!" His voice was hoarse and deep.

She realized the meaning of the hoarseness. She knew by her own feeling that the depth and intensity of his voice was due to the emotion that filled him. She knew she would have found herself voiceless at that moment if she had tried to speak.

"I love you, my darling!" he went on. "I have loved you from the first instant I met you. You have felt it, known it, dear. Have you not?"

She tried to speak, her lips moved, but no sound came from them. But she looked into his eyes, and he read his answer.

With a sweeping gesture of passionate love, he gathered her into his arms and showered kisses upon her lips, her cheeks, her forehead, her hair.

She lay like a stunned thing in his arms. Her joy was almost greater than she could bear. Then as his hot lips sought hers again, she awoke from her semitrance of ecstasy, and with a little sob she flung her arms upward and clasped them about his neck, crying, "Love you, my darling? Love seems too poor a word to express my feeling, for God knows that, save my Lord Jesus, to whom tonight I have fully yielded, you are all my life."

Her voice was stifled with a little rush of tears. Her heart beat with a tumultuous gladness, and her brain throbbed with the wonder of what she conceived to be the honor that had come to her.

"But you are so great—so—" She paused; she could find no words to express all that prospective wifedom to him appeared to her.

He smiled down into her eyes. Her loveliness seemed to him greater than ever before.

"You seem like a king to me!" she gasped at last.

"You, Zillah," he smiled, "are a queen to me. Say, darling, the one word that will fill all my soul with delight—say that you will be mine—and soon, very soon!"

"I will."

He gathered her to himself in an even closer embrace and spent his kisses on her lips.

For a moment, clasped tightly in his arms, she was silent, and he uttered no word. Presently he whispered, "Will it give you joy, I wonder, my darling, to know that I have been a man free of all women's love before? I have seen many women, in many lands, the loveliest of the earth—though none so lovely as you, my sweetheart. It is not egotism on my part, either, to say that many women have sought my love by their smiles and favor. But none ever won a word of love or response from me."

Her eyes, full of rapture, sought his. His were fixed upon her face and filled with a love so great that again she caught her breath in wonder.

"But you, my Zillah, have been to me all that the heart of man could ever wish for, from the first moment I met you. May God give us a long life together, dearest, and make us (with our newborn faith in Him) to be the best, the holiest helpmeets, the one to the other, that this world has ever known."

Where she lay in his arms, he felt her tremble with the intensity of her joy. As he looked down into her deep, dreamy eyes, he saw how they were full of a far-off look, as though she was picturing that united future of which he had spoken.

Perhaps he read that look in her eyes aright. Then as he watched her, he saw how the color deepened in her face. She slowly, proudly, yet with a glad frankness, lifted herself in his arms until, in a tender, passionate caress, her lips rested upon his in the first spontaneous kiss she had given him.

"If the Christ, to whom we have given ourselves tonight, should tarry," she whispered, "and we are spared to dwell together on earth as husband and wife, dear Tom, may God answer all that prayer of yours abundantly."

The cab turned a corner sharply at that moment.

Tom looked through the window. They were within a few hundred yards of where he had given the driver orders to stop. Zillah would have, on alighting, only the length of a short street to traverse before reaching home, and he would take a cab and drive back to the office. But the intervening moments before they would part were very precious, and love took unlimited toll in those swift, fleeting moments.

Chapter 19

ॐ

Tom Hammond Reviewing

That night Tom scarcely slept for the joy of the two loves that had so suddenly come into his life. During the sleepless hours, he learned the true secret of prayer, and that even greater secret, that of communion. Tom, reviewing all that God had revealed to him, learned in those first hours of his new birth the secret of adoring communion with God.

In every way that night was one never to be forgotten by Tom. He needed, too, all the strength born of his new communion with God to meet what awaited him with the coming of the new day's daily papers.

The paper from whose staff he had been practically dismissed in our first chapter (the editor of which was his bitterest enemy) had found how to use "the glass stiletto."

Some of the most scurrilous paragraphs ever

penned appeared in his enemy's columns that morning. It is true that the identity of the man slandered (Tom Hammond) was veiled, but so thinly that every journalist, and a myriad of other readers, would know against whom the utterances were hurled.

Tom would not have been human if the reading of the paragraphs had not hurt him. And he would not have been "partaker of the divine nature," as he now was, if he had not found comfort in the committal of his soreness to God.

"That is the work of that fellow Joyce," he told himself.

Twenty-four hours before, if this utterance had had to have been made by him, he would have said, "That beast Joyce!" But already, as a young soldier of Christ, the promised watch was set upon his lips. In the strength of the two great loves that had come into his life—the love of Christ and the love of Zillah Robart—the scurrilous paragraphs affected him comparatively little.

When he had skimmed the paper and attended to his correspondence and to one or two other special items, he took pen and paper and began to write to his betrothed.

His pen flew over the smooth surface of the paper, but his thoughts were even quicker than his pen. His whole being pulsed with love. He poured out all the wealth of the love of his heart to his beautiful betrothed. When he had finally finished the letter, he sent it by special messenger to Zillah.

He had not forgotten that Major Hadley's second meeting was that day. Three o'clock found him again in the hall. This time it was quite full. There was a new sense of interest, of understanding, within him as he entered the place. This time he bowed his head in real prayer.

This time a lady, a returned Chinese missionary, led in prayer, and then the major resumed his subject.

"We saw, dear friends, at our last meeting," the grand old soldier-preacher began, "what were some of the prophesied signs of our Lord's second coming and how literally these signs were being fulfilled in our midst today. This afternoon I want us to see how He will come; what will happen to the believer; and also what effect the expectancy of His coming should have upon us as believers.

"First of all, how will He come? While Jesus, who had led His disciples out of the city, was in the act of blessing them, He suddenly rose before their eyes, and a cloud received Him out of their sight. He went away in a cloud. The angels, addressing the amazed disciples, declared to them that He would 'so come in like manner as you saw Him go.'

"It may be that to the letter that will be fulfilled, and that our Lord's return for His Church will be in an actual cloud. I think it is probable it will. Anyway, we know that He will come 'in the air,' for Paul, who said, 'Behold, I tell you a mystery: We shall not all sleep, but we shall all be changed, in a moment, in the twinkling of an eye,' when writing more explicitly to the church at Thessalonica, said:

" 'For this we say to you by the word of the Lord, that we who are alive and remain until the coming of the Lord will by no means precede those who are asleep. For the Lord Himself will descend from heaven with a shout, with the voice of an archangel, and with the trumpet of God. And the dead in Christ will rise first. Then we who are alive and remain shall be caught up together with them in the clouds to meet the Lord in the air. And thus we shall always be with the Lord. Therefore comfort one another with these words.'

"Now, beloved, can any words be plainer than these of Paul's? Jesus had Himself said, 'I will come again and receive you to Myself.'

"Now let us look, dear friends, at the separate items of that detailed coming. We have already alluded to the secrecy of the return of our Lord for His people, and people are puzzled over the language used by Paul's description of the return: The Lord shall come 'with a shout.' Then the world at large will hear Him coming? No; we think not. Or, if they hear a sound, they will not understand it.

"The Lord's voice in His spiritual revelations is never heard by anyone but the Lord's people. There were godly shepherds watching their flocks at night, near Bethlehem, and there was a whole host of angels singing, but the Bethlehemites did not hear. No one appears to have heard or seen anything except the godly shepherds. The same, we believe, applies to the 'trumpet,' the call of God. I would emphasize this truth, that it is only the trained ear of the spiritually awakened soul that ever hears the call of God. We believe that all scripture teaches the secrecy as well as the suddenness of the rapture of the Church.

"In all the appearances of the risen, resurrected Lord Jesus, even though, on one occasion at least, He was seen by five hundred disciples at once, yet there is no hint in either the Word of God or the records of history of that time that Jesus was ever seen by the eye of an unbeliever. And depend upon it, no eye will see, no ear will hear Him when He comes again except those who are in Christ.

"When will He come? I do not know; no one knows exactly; but this we do know, from the Word of God—that nothing remains to be fulfilled before He comes. He may come before this meeting closes. Again we know by every sign of the times that His coming cannot now be delayed much longer.

"Now to address a very important feature about the truth of the second coming of the Lord. There are many who argue that such teaching will tend to make the Christian worker careless of his work, his life, etc. There was never a more foolish argument advanced.

"First, take a concrete illustration that gives the flat denial to it—namely, that the most spiritual-minded workers are those whose hearts are saturated with the expectancy of their Lord's near return. Then, too, every such worker finds an incentive to redoubled service in the remembrance that every soul saved through their instrumentality brings the Lord's return nearer—'hastening the coming'—since, when the last unit composing His Church has been gathered in, He will come.

"Scripture is most plain, most emphatic, in its statements that the effect of living in expectancy of our Lord's return touches the spiritual life and service at every point. 'We know,' wrote John, 'that when He is revealed, we shall be like Him, for we shall see Him as He is. And everyone who has this hope in Him purifies himself, just as He is pure.'

"Writing to the Philippians, Paul connects heavenly mindedness with the return of the Lord for His Church, saying, 'Our citizenship is in heaven, from which we also eagerly wait for the Savior, the Lord Jesus Christ.' To the Colossians the great apostle showed how the coming of the Lord was to be the incentive to mortification of self. 'When Christ who is our life appears, then you will also appear with Him in glory. Therefore put to death your members which are on the earth.' James taught that the real cure for impatience was this dwelling in the hope and expectancy of our Lord's coming again. 'You also be patient,' he wrote. 'Establish your hearts, for the coming of the Lord is at hand.'

"The great stimulator, too, of Christian diligence is to be found in the coming of the Lord. Peter wrote, 'But the day of the Lord will come as a thief in the night. . . Therefore, since all these things will be dissolved, what manner of persons ought you to be in holy conduct and godliness, looking for and hastening the coming. . . . Therefore, beloved, looking forward to these things, be diligent to be found by Him in peace, without spot and blameless.'

"May I say, too, in all gentleness and love, that it has seemed to me for years that the missing link in all so-called holiness preaching is this much neglected expectancy of our Lord's return. Paul connects holiness and the second coming of Christ in his first Epistle to the Thessalonians, saying, 'May the God of peace Himself sanctify you completely; and may your whole spirit, soul, and body be preserved blameless at the coming of our Lord Jesus Christ.'

"The scoffing of the world against us as Christians is that the professed bond of love is absent from our lives. And here again God's Word shows us that a real living in expectancy of our Lord's return would teach us to love one another.

"I must close, friends. But before I do, let me beseech every Christian here this afternoon to get alone with God and His Word. Assure yourself that Jesus is coming again, that He is coming soon, and that you are so living that you will 'not be ashamed. . . at His coming.'"

Chapter 20

❧

"MY MENTOR"

About the hour that Tom entered the hall to listen to the major's second address, Cohen, the Jew, was in his workshop, his brain busy with many problems, while his hands worked on the wonderful temple work.

The door opened quietly, and Zillah entered. She often came for a talk with him at this hour, as she was mostly sure of an uninterrupted conversation.

The young Jew gave the beautiful girl a pleasant greeting. Then after the exchange of a few general words, the pair was silent. Zillah broke the silence at last:

"Abraham," she began, "I want to talk to you on—on—well—I've something important to say."

He eyed her curiously, a tender little smile moving about among the lines of his mouth. There was a new note in her voice, a new light in her eyes. He had caught glimpses of both when they had met at breakfast and again at dinner, but both were more marked than ever now.

He had laid down his tool at her first word. Now she laid one of her pretty, plump hands on his as she went on: "You could not have been kinder, truer, dear Abraham, if you had been my own brother. I have looked upon you as a brother, as a friend, as a protector, and I have always felt that I could, and would, make a confidant of you, should the need ever arise."

The gentle smile in his eyes as well as on his mouth encouraged her, and she went on: "A gentlemen has asked me to marry him, Abraham—"

Cohen gave a quick little start.

"I have promised," she continued, "for I love him, and he loves me as only—"

"Who is he, Zillah?"

"Mr. Hammond!"

His eyes flashed with the mildest surprise. But to her astonishment, she noticed that he showed no anger.

In spite of all his usual gentleness, she had half expected a little outburst.

"He is of the Gentile race, Zillah!" Cohen said quietly.

She noticed that he said *race* and not *faith*, and she unconsciously took courage from the fact.

She was silent for a moment. Her lips moved slightly, but no sound came from her. Watching her, he wondered. She was praying!

Suddenly she lifted her head. She allowed her eyes to meet his as she said, "Abraham! I have found the Messiah! He whom the Gentiles call the Christ, the man-God, Jesus, *is* the Messiah!"

His eyes were fixed on her face. She was surprised that there was neither anger nor indignation in them.

"May I tell you why I think, why I *know* He is the Messiah, Abraham?" she asked.

"Do, Zillah!"

He spoke very gently, and she wondered more and more. She began to pour out her soul in the words of the Old Testament scriptures, connecting them with their fulfillment in the New Testament.

"Now I know, dear Abraham," she cried, "how it is that Jehovah is allowing our rabbis to be led to dates that prove that Messiah is coming soon. *Now* I know why God has allowed our nation to be stirred up. It is because the Christ *is* coming.

"Only it is not as the Messiah of the Jews that He comes soon—He came thus more than nineteen hundred years ago. This time, when He comes, He will come for His Church, His redeemed one—Jew and Gentile alike who are washed in His blood that was shed on Calvary for all the human race. For He was surely *God's* Lamb and was slain at the Great, the last real Passover if only we all—our race—could see this. What the blood of that first Passover lamb in Egypt was in type, to our people in their bondage and blood deliverance, so Jesus was in reality.

"And now, dear Abraham, that same Jesus has not

only blotted out all my sin, but He bids me look for Him to come again. When *next* He comes—it may be before even this day closes—"

Cohen shot a quick, puzzled glance at her. She did not notice it but went on: "I have learned many things from the scriptures since I have been going to the little room at Spitalfields, and from the *Word* of Jehovah Himself I have learned that Jesus may now come at any moment.

"He will come in the air and will catch away all His believing children. Then, as the teachers show from the Word of God, when the Church is gone, there shall arise a terrible power, a man who will be Satan's great agent to lead the whole world astray— *Anti*christ, the Word of God calls him—then during a period, probably about seven years altogether, there shall be an ever-growing persecution of those who shall witness boldly for Jesus, and—"

"*Who* will *they* be, Zillah," he interrupted, "if all the Church, as you say, will be taken out of the world at the coming of Christ?"

"One of the teachers the other night said that the natural consequence of the sudden taking away of the believers from this earth would probably be, at first, a mighty revival, a turning to God. If this be so, then these converts will be the witnesses to Jesus during the awful seven years, which the Word of God calls the Great Tribulation.

"Then, too, one of the teachers said, 'It is possible that not all Christians will be caught up in the air at the coming again of Jesus, but *only* those faithful ones who are found watching, expecting His coming.' If that be so, then there will be thousands of Christians left behind who will have to pass through the awful time of Antichrist's tribulation."

Her face glowed with holy light as she went on: "At first, our own race will return to Jerusalem, and to all the land of our Father, still believing in the coming of the Messiah. The temple—that wondrous temple for which you are working—will be raised to Jehovah. The morning and evening sacrifices will be resumed. Then the Antichrist will make our people believe that he is the Messiah. Pretending to be Israel's friend and protector, he will deceive them at first, but by and by, he will try to force idolatry upon them; he will want to set up in our glorious temple an idol, an abomination. The great mass of our people, in the land of our fathers, will blindly accept this hideous idol worship.

"But Jehovah will not let Antichrist have his own way completely. Jesus, with all those who were caught up with Him into the air, will come to the deliverance of our people. He will come, *this* time, to the earth. He will fight against Antichrist, will overcome him; His feet will stand on the Mount of Olives.

"Our poor deluded, suffering people will see Him, as our own prophets have said: 'I will pour on the house of David and on the inhabitants of Jerusalem the Spirit of grace and supplication; then they will look on Me whom they pierced. Yes, they will mourn for Him as one mourns for his only son, and grieve for Him as one grieves for a firstborn.'"

She paused abruptly, struck by Cohen's quiet manner, where she had expected a storm. Gazing wonderingly into his face, she cried, "Abraham, why are you so quiet? Why have you not cursed me? Can it be that you, too, know about these glorious truths?"

There was sadness and kindness in his eyes as he returned her pleading glance. But there was no trace of anger.

"I wonder why, little sister," he began, "I am not angry, as the men of Israel's faith usually are, even though the defaulter should be as beautiful as Zillah Robart."

His glance grew kinder as he went on: "I began to wonder where my little sister went, twice a week, in the evenings, and was anxious about her, lest she, in her innocence of heart and ignorance of life, should get into trouble. I followed her one night and saw that she entered a hall, which I knew to be a preaching place for Jews.

"I did not enter the place myself, but that very first night, while waiting about for a few minutes, I met an old friend, a Jew like myself, by *race*, but a Christian by faith. He talked with me, pointed to *our* scriptures, quoted from the Gentile New Testament, showed from them how, in every detail, the birth, the life, the death of Jesus the Nazarene fulfilled the prophecies of our Father, and—"

"And you, Abraham, you see that Jesus was the Messiah?"

Slowly, almost sorrowfully it seemed to the eager girl, he shook his head.

"I cannot say all that, Zillah. I sat in a seat last night in that hall, where I could see you and Hammond, where I could hear all that was said upon the platform, but where I knew that neither you nor Hammond would be able to see me. All that I heard last night has more than half convinced me, but—well, I cannot rush through this matter. I have to remember that it has to do with the life beyond, as well as this life.

"I saw the meeting between Hammond and you, Zillah. I had before begun to sense something of Hammond's probable feelings for you, and I had seen you look at him in a way that, though you did not yourself probably realize it, meant, I knew, a growing feeling for him warmer than our maidens usually bestow on a Gentile. I saw you enter the cab together and drive off, and—"

He sighed. Then without finishing his sentence, he said, "Perhaps I shall see with you soon. Meanwhile, dear—"

He lifted his hands, let them rest upon her head, and softly, reverently cried, "The Lord bless you and keep you; the Lord make His face shine upon you, and be gracious to you; the Lord lift up His countenance upon you, and give you peace."

The sweet old Nazarite blessing never fell more tenderly upon human ears than it did upon Zillah Robart. Jehovah *had* been very gracious to her. She had feared anger, indignation from her brother-in-law; she received blessing instead.

As he slowly lifted his hands from her head, she caught them in hers, lifted them to her lips, and kissed them gratefully.

"May that blessing fall back upon your own head, upon your heart, your life, dear Abraham!" she cried.

Still holding his hands, she lifted her head. An eager light filled her face as she added: "It is only a few days till Passover. I shall pray God that He will reveal Jesus fully to you before that!"

She dropped his hands and made for the door. "I hear the children from school," she cried. Then she was gone.

Cohen did not turn to his work. But taking a New Testament from his pocket, he began to study anew the Passion of Jesus as recorded in the Gospels.

Chapter 21

❧

Was He Mad?

Madge, a wife of barely eighteen hours, found her husband's church packed in every nook and corner when she entered it on Sunday morning.

The news of her sudden return and equally sudden marriage had helped to fill the church, though the knowledge that the Reverend Doig was to preach would, in itself, have been sufficient to have gathered an unusually large congregation.

During the pastor's sickness the pulpit had been filled by various good men, secured by the deacons from all over the country. Doig had preached twice before and was already a great favorite with the people.

The pastor had not been well enough to be present at any service for many weeks, and as he entered the church this morning, leaning heavily upon his wife's arm, he received quite an ovation from the people.

In spite of the curiosity and excitement over

Madge's appearance, the congregation speedily settled down to quiet worship. There was something quieting in the preacher's manner.

After singing a hymn, a deep solemnity came down upon the assembly. It deepened as the preacher unfolded the wonder of the Bible revelation relating to the Lord's Second Coming.

Madge forgot her husband as she drank in the glorious truth. Had she been more alert in watching the pastor, she would have seen how restless he grew! How angrily his eyes flashed! How scowling his brows became.

Some of the people noticed their pastor's evident displeasure, and so did one or two of the deacons. But no one dreamed that he would dare to utter any dissent.

Was he mad? Perhaps he was, for the time, nursing a groundless, senseless anger and jealousy. He was jealous of this man's hold upon the people. He had not dreamed that any man could hold his congregation as this man was holding them. He was angry, too, at the doctrine preached.

With a startling suddenness he leaped to his feet, forgetting his weakness as he cried, "I will not have that lying, senseless nonsense preached in *my* church, Mr. Doig. You will either announce another text and take a different subject, sir, or you must cease to preach!"

A slight flush rose into the cheeks of the preacher as he turned to the pastor, and in a low but firm voice he said:

"Dear pastor, if you insist, I will desist. But I cannot, if I preach on, do other than declare all that God would have me do. Why, even as we are here, our loving Lord may come, and if I faltered in my testimony, I should have to meet Him ashamedly—and—"

"Rot!" muttered the pastor. The word was heard by everyone, and a murmur of strong dissent ran through the place.

With a white, angry face and flashing, savage eyes, the pastor walked to the table and leaned upon it heavily with his weakness as he cried hoarsely, "This service is now concluded. While I hold the pastorate, no such sentimental rubbish as Mr. Doig seems bent upon giving us will be voiced from this platform."

One of the deacons protested. The pastor was firm. Passion had rendered him temporarily irresponsible. Another of the deacons urged the people to disperse quietly.

Doig walked down to one of the deacons and whispered, "If I go at once, it will help matters." The pair then left the church. The congregation followed quickly. The deacons remained behind to confer together over the situation, which was of a hitherto unheard-of character.

The pastor had left by the side door, and leaning more heavily than ever upon Madge, they made their way to the house of Madge's father. They were staying there. They took a private way, by which they were spared the unpleasantness of meeting any of the congregation.

Four minutes took them to the house. Neither of them spoke during the brief journey. For the first time in her life, Madge knew what it was to feel the touch of fear. She had married the man by her side knowing comparatively little of his real character and temperament.

There may be insanity in his family, she mused as she walked by his side. She had already told herself that nothing but a temporary touch of madness could have led to his outburst in the church.

Arrived at the house, the pastor went straight to his room; this gave Madge an opportunity to confer with her father and mother a moment.

"His long, anxious illness has unsettled his brain a little!" her mother said.

"The best thing will be to take no notice; let us all be as cheerful, as much like our ordinary selves, as we can. Then, if we can persuade him to go away tomorrow, I guess the best thing for you to do, Madge, will be to get a good doctor to examine him and prescribe for him."

The dinner meal that followed presently was fairly free of constraint. After dinner, Mr. and Mrs. Finisterre slipped away and left the husband and wife to themselves.

Almost immediately after the pair left, the pastor began to abuse the preacher of the morning and to denounce the teachings of the Lord's Second Coming.

"But, my dear," cried Madge, "it is evidently almost the most prominent doctrine in the New Testament. There are more direct references to it in the New Testament, Mr. Doig said, than to any other revealed doctrine."

"But it's not *my* doctrine," snapped the pastor, "not the doctrine of *our* church. It was scoffed at our college when *I* was a student, and—and—"

Madge gazed wonderingly at him. His argument seemed so immature, if not actually sinful.

"But," she cried, "I don't see how that argument holds. To me, it sounds like blasphemy almost to say, '*I*, as a *minister*, and *we*, as a *church*, will not preach the most prominent doctrine of the New Testament because of the foolish abuse of the teaching by a few wild visionaries who let their fancy run away with their judgment.' "

The pastor gazed at her in amazement. Her fashion of putting the matter gave him little opportunity to reply, so he took refuge in the coarse sneer, "Have you turned *Doigite*?"

With a quick flush in her cheeks and sudden flashing of eye, Madge replied, "If by that you mean do I see and have I accepted the revelation of the Word of God regarding the near coming of Christ, then I say 'Yes.' I am *not* a Doigite, but I am, thank God, a Christ-ian! A very young one, a very poor and inexperienced one, 'tis true, but still I am one and am desirous to live for the Lord to whom I have given myself, and after all I heard from the preacher this morning, I am more than ever determined to serve Christ wholly, and I can quite see how this wondrous *fact* of the near return of our Lord will be a new and mighty force to revolutionize all my life."

An ugly snarl curled the lips of the pastor, and he was just beginning a cruel little speech when one of the deacons was announced.

Madge left the two men alone. As she passed on to her own room, there was a terrible pain at her heart, for the hideous thought came to her: *Can Homer be truly converted? If he is, how can it be that he flatly refuses to believe what God has so plainly revealed?*

Chapter 22

❧

FROM THE PROPHET'S CHAMBER

Tom was alone in his editorial office. He had come to the day, the moment at last, when he felt constrained to write out of his full heart, to the readers of his paper, all that he yearned that the world should know of the imminence of the return of the Lord.

Before he put pen to paper to write on this supreme theme in his "Prophet's Chamber" column, he bowed his head on his desk and prayed for guidance. Then he began to write out his heart fully, telling first of his conversion and of the meeting conducted by Major Hadley.

His whole being was fired with holy purpose. "Has any preacher ever had such a pulpit as has the editor of *The Courier*?" he wrote. "Has any preacher ever had so mighty a privilege, so great a responsibility as is mine today? This paper circulates through more than a million people's hands, even allowing that only the one person purchasing the paper reads it—though one might almost safely double that million, since there are very few of the papers that will not be read by *two* or more persons.

"As a converted editor of the great daily, I have put my hand, my pen, my mind into the mighty, unerring hand of God, praying that I may write only that which will reach the *hearts* of my readers. And the question comes to me, 'What word does London, does England, most need today?'

"This—that all the world should know, and realize, that any day, indeed, any hour, Christ may return—not to the earth but *into the air*—"

Here followed the teaching of the Gospel and Epistles, as he had learned it from Major Hadley and from his own subsequent personal study of the Word of God.

"I appeal to the most thoughtful of my readers, I appeal to the unthinking, as I say, 'Do you not see how a real belief in this near coming of Christ would revolutionize all our national, commercial, domestic, and church life? How, too, it would immediately settle every social problem.'

"If our legislators realized that before the present parliamentary session could end in the ordinary way, that Christ might come, what a speedy end they would seek to put to every national iniquity.

"The hideous drink traffic would be swept from our land. And in sweeping that curse away, the awful problem of the unemployed, the homeless, the starving, our national poverty would be swept away.

"The shameful opium traffic with China; the national greed for territory; the traffic in white slaves; and every other national iniquity would be abolished.

"Christian churches (so-called) would become worthy of the name *Christian*. All those bits of devilish device used to extract and extort money from the pockets of the people would end. Theatricals would be left to the theaters; entertainments would be left to the music halls; the Church would leave all these things to their master—*the devil*.

"In *social* life, people would pay their debts; the sinful extravagance that marks the life of today would cease. Christians would love one another. Every evangelical denomination would be inter-denominational in the truest sense and be one wholly in their crucified, risen, coming Lord. A love for the poor fallen world, such as has never been since our Lord spent Himself in service, would be the order of the day and not the vision of a few. Every missionary society would have more men and women and money than they actually needed.

"But even as I pen this millennium-like picture, I know, from the Word of God, that it *cannot* be *before* Christ comes. But I seek to arouse every *Christian* to God's call to them on this matter. You who profess to be Christ's dare not refuse this truth.

"The vast bulk of the churches preach that the world will continually improve until the earth shall be fit for Christ to come and reign. But I defy any cleric or layman to show me a single word of scripture that gives the faintest color to that belief or statement.

"Things (spiritual) are growing worse and worse, proving the truth of the New Testament prophecies, 'Perilous times will come.' 'Evil men and imposters will grow worse and worse, *deceiving* and *being deceived*.' If only we could all be induced to read the signs of the times in the light of scripture! We should then realize that we were in the thickest darkness of the world's blackest night, the darkness immediately preceding the dawn, and we should be looking for 'the Morning Star.' "

Here, writing with swift, eager pen, he went over the ground covered by Major Hadley regarding the signs of the coming of the Lord. Then the increased effort in the foreign mission fields. The growth of the spirit of lawlessness in the world, in the Church. The multiplicity of spiritualistic devices—*doctrine of devils*. The awakening of all real, true, spiritually minded Bible students to the fact of Christ's near return.

"He *will* come! He is near at hand! Every sign of the times proclaims this! It is night now, and He 'will come as a thief in the night.' At any moment now we may look for Him. Before this news sheet, damp from the press, is in the hands of my readers, Christ *may* have come and taken away *every one* of His own believing people—*I* shall be missing; another here and another there will be missing.

"And when a puzzled, troubled London will be

gathering in business, that saying shall have come to pass, 'One will be taken and the other left!'

"May every Christian be ready to meet his Lord, when He shall come, and every unready, unsaved soul who reads these 'Prophet's Chamber' columns seek the face of God through faith in the atoning work of Jesus Christ. For, believe me, His return is very near; to some of us the sound of His footfalls is even now in our ears."

He bent his head over the written sheets, praying God to bless the message. Then an interruption came. A knock at the door, and Ralph Bastin entered.

Chapter 23

❧

Passover!

Cohen, the Jew, blew out the candle and set the stand aside. The knees of his trousers were pressed and dusty. He had just been over the whole house, lighted candle in hand, and had searched every nook and cranny for the faintest sign of leaven in the form of bread, cake, or biscuit crumb. He had found nothing and went to his room to bathe and change his clothing.

"What of you, Zillah?" he had asked the lovely girl earlier in the day. "With your newly espoused faith in the Nazarene, shall you partake of the lamb with us?"

"Certainly, I will," she replied. "Only I shall take the meal more in the spirit of the Lord's Supper of the Christian Church. And, Abraham, all the time I shall be praying that you may meet the Christ of God, Jesus of Nazareth; and while you seek to remember our people's deliverance from the land of bondage, I shall be praying that you may be delivered from the bondage of the legalism of our race."

The Passover table was spread in Cohen's house. The table had an egg according to rabbinical order, and there was a tiny roast lamb as well. There was the glass dish of bitter herbs; the salt water, typifying the tears of Israel's misery in Egypt; a dish of almonds, apples, and other fruit, chopped and mixed, representing the lime and mortar of the brick making in the land of bondage.

Chervil and parsley were there, and lettuce. A large pile of unleavened cakes, a big colored glass ewer with unfermented wine and water, and many other items considered to be the orthodox thing at the feast.

All the Cohen household was there. Zillah was radiant with the glow of the new life in Christ that had come to her.

Leah, her sister, was red-eyed and sullen. Zillah had been pleading with her to open her mind and her heart to the Christian teaching of the Messiah who had come and who had atoned for *all* the race, Jews and Gentiles alike.

Angry and sullen, the wife had said hard things of Zillah. Her frivolous, irresponsible nature was more than satisfied with the barest form of the faith of her race.

The two children were full of suppressed excitement, the elder—the boy—especially.

Cohen, the head of the house, was singularly quiet and grave. His eyes had a faraway look in them.

He looked like a man moving in a trance.

Presently the boy asked, according to the usual formula: "What do you mean, Father, by this service?"

Cohen's eyes stared over the head of his son, and in a voice very unlike its usual tones, replied: "It is the sacrifice of Jehovah's Passover, who halted by the blood-sprinkled houses of our fathers in Egypt, that the destroying angel should come not nigh, when He smote the Egyptians but preserved our fathers."

"Will our people *ever* do this, Father?" queried the boy.

"Till Messiah come, they will, dear son."

"*When* will Messiah come, Father?" continued the boy.

"*Tonight*, perhaps, my son. Set His chair! Open the door!"

Swiftly but quietly the boy placed a chair at the table then set the door wide open and left it thus and returned to his place by the table.

Leah took the ewer and poured out a little wine and water into each glass. Each took up their glass and drank from the first cup of blessing.

There was a moment's pause, then Cohen spread his hands, bowed his head, and repeated "the Blessing": "The Lord bless us and keep us; the Lord make His face shine upon us and be gracious unto us. The Lord lift up the light of his countenance upon us and give us peace."

Under her breath, yet distinctly heard by Cohen, in the solemn hush that followed the Blessing, Zillah murmured: "*But now in Christ Jesus you who once were far off have been brought near by the blood of Christ. For He Himself is our peace.*"

Cohen glanced quietly at her. She met the glance with one of intense yearning. He translated it rightly as meaning, "If *only* you could see this truth!"

There were two bowls of water set on a sideboard. Cohen and his wife rinsed their hands in one bowl, Zillah and the two children in the other.

Then the first Hallel was repeated—Psalms 113 and 114. The second cup of blessing was taken by each. Then Cohen asked a blessing on each kind of food on the table. Then he carved a portion of lamb for each one, they took their seats, and the meal began.

The children were excused from eating the stinging bitter herbs. But Cohen, Leah, and Zillah each took a little with their lamb and unleavened bread.

Conversation became fairly general over the meal, except that Leah's sullen anger increased, and she kept silent.

At the conclusion of the meal, the third cup of blessing was drunk, and Cohen repeated Psalms 115, 116, 117, and 118. At the close of the Hallel, the fourth and last cup of blessing was taken. The feast was over.

A sudden silence fell upon them all. No one moved, no one spoke, for a moment. Suddenly Zillah broke the dead silence. She had a glorious voice, and she let it ring out in that wondrous song:

"Not all the blood of beasts
On Jewish altars stain
Could give the guilty conscience peace,
Or wash away our stain."

No one interrupted. Cohen *could* not, for the thrall of some strange, new power was upon him. His wife was furious—but kept her fury bottled up. The children were delighted; they loved to hear their aunt sing, and to the amazement of their father and mother, they joined in the singing, for, with other children, they had often of late been to the evening meeting for Jewish children. And Zillah, who had talked with them, believed that they loved the Christ.

Without a break, the three voices sang on:

"But Christ the Heavenly Lamb,
Take all our sins away;
A sacrifice of nobler name
And richer Blood than they.

"My faith would lay her hand
On that meek head of Thine,
While as a penitent I stand,
And here confess my sin.

"My soul looks back to see
The burden Thou didst bear

When Hanging on the accursed tree,
And knows her guilt was there.

"Believing, we rejoice
To feel the curse remove;
We bless the Lamb with cheerful voice,
And trust His bleeding love."

Again, for a full thirty seconds, as the glorious song finished, there was an absolute silence, save for the creaking of Leah's chair as she moved in petty anger on her seat.

Zillah had kept her eyes fixed upon Cohen's face all the time she was singing and had seen a strangely wondrous light slowly gather in his eyes. She had known for days that he was very near to the point of acceptance of Christ. Even as they had gathered at the table of the Passover, she was not sure but that in all but profession and testimony, he was a Christian.

Now he suddenly broke the silence:

"Sing the last two verses again, Zillah," he said.

Zillah's glorious voice rang out. And now, even to *her* wonder, Cohen's deeper tones joined hers. Her heart leaped as she noted the emphasis he put upon the "*my* soul."

She sang on. His voice sang on, too. Then came the last verse, and in a perfect burst of triumph, his voice rang out. It was a strangely ecstatic moment for Zillah. Tears flooded her eyes; she tried to speak, but her emotion choked her.

Cohen stood up. His face was ablaze with the wonder of the revelation that had come to him. He spread his hands upward, and his eyes were lifted in the same direction as he cried:

"Loving Christ! Precious Jesus! I am *Yours*— Yours—YOURS—!"

Then he remembered his wife.

"Leah, wife of my heart. Jesus is the Messiah! Leah, dear heart," he cried as he moved to her side.

"Bah!" she cried. With a thrust of her hand and foot, she kept him from her.

He bent over her very tenderly, stooping to meet her eyes and trying to take her hand.

The two children clung to Zillah, and the boy suddenly began to pipe out, in his clear treble, the hymn so beloved of Jewish children who attended the mission meetings:

> *"Come to the Savior,*
> *Make no delay."*

Leah shot a fierce, angry glance in the boy's direction, then without looking at her husband, she thrust at him, to prevent his taking her hand, as she cried, "Accursed! Don't touch *me!*"

"But, Leah!" he began tenderly.

She flung herself sharply upon him and spat in his face. Then she turned sharply from him again.

A full half minute went by. The room was so eerily still that it startled her. She turned to gaze where the four had been.

The room was empty except for herself!

With a cry she started to her feet. They could not have gone out the door, for her chair had all the time stood right in the way. What was this then that had happened?

Her breath came hot and labored. A reeling sickness began to steal over her. She dropped back, terrified, into her chair, gasping, "Zillah said this morning, 'The Christ will come *soon*, *suddenly*, then those who are His will be taken, unseen, unheard, from the world!' "

With a sharp, anguished cry, she let her terror-filled eyes sweep the room again as she cried, "And my *children*, too!"

Her eyes were tearless, but dry, hard sobs shook her frame.

The next moment a kind of frenzy seized her. She rushed to the front door and into the street. She would find out if anyone else was missing.

A little crowd was on the pavement. A cab stood by the curb. A minister of some kind was standing on the front board. He glanced up at the driver's seat as he cried, "But someone, surely, must have seen what became of him. If he fell off his box in a fit, where is his body?"

"I seed him one hinstant," cried a voice from the crowd. "I wur looking straight at 'im, 'cos I sed to myself, taint often as yer see a kebby wear a white 'at, nowadays. Then while I wur starin' at 'im, he sort o' disappeared, the reins fell on the roof o' the keb, the 'oss stopped, an—"

"He's gone!" shrieked a woman's voice.

It was Leah. Bare-headed, dressed in all her festal finery, she had just rushed down the steps of the house and heard the question and answer as to the disappearance of the cabdriver. The crowd turned and faced her; her shrill tones had startled them.

"He's gone to Jehovah!" she screamed again. "My husband, my sister, my two children—we were at Passover—we—"

With a piercing shriek she flung up her arms, laughed hideously, and fell in a huddled heap on the bottom step of the flight.

Chapter 24

❧

"THAT SAYING SHALL
HAVE COME TO PASS"

Tom greeted Ralph heartily. Ralph had been away in Paris for two weeks, partly on business, partly for a change.

As soon as their greetings were exchanged, he turned eagerly to Tom as he said, "But I say, old man, what on earth is all this jargon you wrote me about, the return of the Christ and such?"

Tom replied, "I have been so impressed with the necessity of speaking to the world on this momentous subject that I have made it the subject of my 'Prophet's Chamber' column."

He gathered up the sheets he had written and passed them over the table to Ralph.

"You will see I have written it in the simplest style, Ralph," he said. "I wanted it to be a man's quiet, earnest, simple utterance to his fellow man, not a journalist's article."

Ralph's eyes raced over the papers. His face was a strange study while he read, reflecting different emotions. As he finished the last sheet, he searched Tom's face.

"My dear Tom," he began. His voice was very grave. "You'll ruin *The Courier*! You will ruin yourself! The world will call you mad—"

"They called my Lord mad, Ralph, and they have called His servants mad, over and over again, ever since. The Word of our God tells us that Christ said: 'Whoever confesses Me before men, him I will also confess before My Father who is in heaven. . . . If anyone desires to come after Me, let him deny himself, and take up his cross, and follow Me. For whoever desires to save his life will lose it, but whoever loses his life for My sake will find it. For what profit is it to a man if he gains the whole world, and loses his own soul. . . . For whoever is ashamed of Me and My words, of him the Son of Man will be ashamed when He comes in His own glory, and in His Father's, and of the holy angels.' "

Tom leaned forward in his chair to lay his hand on the wrist of the other, to plead with him. But with an exclamation of angry impatience, Ralph cried, "Hang it, old man, you must be going dotty!"

With an expression of annoyance, almost amounting to disgust, he swung around on his heel.

"Look here, Tom," he began.

He swirled back to meet his friend face-to-face.

Then with a startled cry, he stared at the chair in

which, an instant before, Tom had been sitting.

The chair was empty!

"Good God!" he gasped.

Instinctively he knew what had happened! He recalled the closing words of Tom's article, which he had just read:

"That saying shall have come to pass, 'ONE WILL BE TAKEN AND THE OTHER LEFT.'"

A strange, unnatural trembling seized him. He dropped into the chair he had been occupying and stared at the empty revolving chair opposite.

"Good—God!"

For a time he sat still and silent like a man stunned. Then as his eyes traveled slowly to where the article lay, he smiled wearily, drew the papers toward him, and took his pen from his pocket. He began to write after the last words penned by his translated chief:

"P.S.—Written by the subeditor of *The Courier*. By the time this printed sheet is being read, the world will have learned that a section of the community has been suddenly taken from our midst. The editor of *The Courier*, the giant mind and kindly heart of Tom Hammond, have been taken from us.

"The writer of this postscript, who was in the room when the 'Prophet' of *The Courier* was taken, was in the act of scorning his message as to the nearing of the great translation. 'In a moment, in the twinkling of an eye,' he was gone.

"The writer has not left the room since and has no

means of knowing who else among those known to him are missing—not many *personal* acquaintances, he fears, since one's personal clique has never shown any very marked signs of what one has hitherto considered an ultra type of Christianity.

"When we pass out of this room, presently, and touch the great outside world once more, what shall we find? How soon will it be generally known that a section of the community—a larger section, maybe, than we conceive possible—has been silently, suddenly, secretly taken from our midst? What will follow? Where are the prophets who shall teach us where we are and what we may expect? Does the end of the world follow next? Is there any order of events, specified in the Bible, that follows this mysterious translation? If so, what is it? Who will show us these things?

"Again, since I, the writer of this postscript, am left, while my friend Hammond is taken, why am I left, and why shall I find—as of course I will when I begin to go out among my acquaintances—hundreds of others left? I have been christened and confirmed. I have always supposed myself a Christian by virtue of these things, to which a clean, decent life has been added. Thousands upon thousands, I feel sure, will be puzzled by this same contemplation when this wonderful translation becomes generally known.

"If we are not made Christians by christening and confirmation, why have we always been taught so by our clergy? How many of these same clergy shall we find left behind?"

There came a tap at the door. The messenger boy, Charlie, appeared. He glanced toward the empty editor's chair then stammered, "I beg pardon, sir. I thought Mr. Hammond was here, sir. I was checking to see if the 'Prophet's' column was ready."

Gathering up the sheets of paper, he clipped them together, stamped them with Tom's mechanical imprinter, and handed the sheaf to the lad, giving him instructions to deliver them to the composing room.

As the lad left the room, Ralph sat back in his chair and tried to think out the position of affairs. Suddenly he started to his feet, wild of eye and with horror in his face.

"Viola?" he muttered. "My beautiful little Viola? She has talked continuously of the Christ of late. Has she been—?"

He seized his hat, and with a sob of fear, he rushed away.

Outside the office he came upon a cab. He leaped into it, shouting the Bloomsbury address to the man.

"Drive for your life!" he yelled. "A sovereign for you if you get me there quickly!"

The man's horse was fresh. They rushed through the streets. Arriving at the house, he tossed the driver his promised sovereign, and letting himself in with his latchkey, he dashed into the drawing room. It was empty!

He was leaving the room hurriedly when he encountered the landlady. "Miss Viola has gone to bed, sir. She overtired herself, visiting the sick poor with her flowers and all that today, and she—"

"Thanks!" With a hurried nod he raced up the stairs. The child's bedroom was next to his own. He entered it without knocking.

The room was in darkness. He lit the lamp then shot a quick glance at the bed. In that first glance, he saw that it was empty. He went close to the bed; it had been occupied, he could see that.

"God help me!" he groaned. And two great tears fell glittering from his eyes.

"Viola! Viola, my precious darling!" he moaned. "You were my life, my—"

His emotions choked him. He dropped into the chair next to the bed, buried his face in the pillow, and wept.

For five minutes he remained thus. Then rousing himself, he muttered, "I must play the man and get back to the office and lay hold of things."

He left the room and managed to leave the house without encountering his landlady. Lucky in finding a cab, he had himself driven first to the central news agency. He wanted to find out if anything of the mystery was generally known.

"If the world has to go on, for a time, just as it *has* been doing, in spite of this wonderful thing," he muttered, "then as acting editor of *The Courier*, I had better stifle every feeling, save the professional, and give London—England—the best morning issue under the new condition of things."

Chapter 25

❧

FOILED!

Thin and pale, but with the likeness of God shining in her dark eyes, Mrs. Joyce sat wearily stitching at her warehouse needlework.

Jem Joyce, the drunken, reprobate husband, was serving a six-week sentence for his old crime, drunken disorderliness in the streets and assaulting the police. His time would soon be up. The fear-filled wife had recalled the fact that very day, though she could not be sure of the actual date.

As she worked now her voice whispered low in song. Low, soft, yearning in its passionate longing for her Lord's return, she began again to hum when a step sounded somewhere near. She turned deadly pale. She recognized the step. It was her husband's.

She had just time to drop back into her chair and, trembling, resume her work when the brute entered. He was drunk—viciously, murderously drunk.

He began to curse her the moment he crossed the threshold. He called her foul names. He sneered at her religion and blasphemed the name of her Lord.

Her lips moved, but no sound came from them. She prayed for grace to be silent, for she feared she might aggravate him. Suddenly he shook his fist in her face and hissed, "Curse you! Do you know I've only come back to you to settle all my scores? I've come to—"

His foaming, blaspheming rage choked him, and he leaped forward and caught her by the throat.

She could not cry out. She thought he was going to strangle her. Then he drew himself up, and drawing her toward himself at the same time, he hurled himself forward to dash her head against the wall of the room.

It was *his* head that struck the wall. His hands clutched air. He fell headlong, stunned, bleeding, and—presently, he was dead.

The room was very still.

Margaret Joyce was in the air, with her Lord!

Chapter 26

❧

DISQUALIFIED

Madge and her husband left Albany on the Monday morning, ostensibly for a brief honeymoon but chiefly with a view to recruit her husband's health. They had gone to a tiny little house in the Catskills.

The heart of Madge was broken, for her husband would not be friendly with her. He was barely civil when he spoke to her and answered her in short, sharp monosyllables only. All her old natural pride was, fortunately for *him*, swallowed up in her newfound faith in God and her surrender to Him. And with this there had come to her the patience and purifying, born of the hope of the near return of the Lord.

She had been alone, thinking over the whole position, for a couple of hours. The situation had become intolerable. She determined to make an appeal to him, though it hurt her natural pride even to contemplate it.

"Help me! Teach me! Guide me!" she cried to God. And in the strength of the divine promises of upholding and guidance, she decided to go to her husband.

He was alone, with a book before him on the table. But he was not reading. He was not even thinking. His mind was in a confused whirl. He had made a fool of himself in public. He knew it, and he had been too proud to apologize. He had spurned and snubbed the woman for whom he had professed to be dying of love and who had made the greatest sacrifice any honest woman can make to man—since she had offered herself to him in marriage.

He knew that in the eyes of his wife, and in the eyes of the little world he had lived and labored in, he had lowered himself.

Some of his own recent platform and pulpit utterances returned to his mind, and they stung him. It was at the worst of all moments for her mission of reconciliation that Madge entered the room.

With a rare gentleness she began to plead with him, reminding him of all the passionate love he had expressed for her up to the very moment almost when they entered the church together for that Sunday morning service.

He answered her coldly, sullenly at first. Then he grew pettishly angry with her and snapped sharply at her, contradicting her in nearly everything she said.

"But, Homer," she pleaded again, kneeling before him and trying to take his hand.

With an angry exclamation, he rose sharply to his feet and thrust her away with his foot as he cried, "I don't want you! You go your way, I'll go mine, and—"

He stopped suddenly. With a sharp cry of agony, he stretched his hands out into the empty space, where an instant before, she had knelt—for in one flashing moment, she had disappeared from before his eyes.

"Madge! Madge, dear love, dear love, dear wife!" he cried.

Deep down in his heart, he knew what had happened—only he would not admit it to himself.

He flashed a swift glance at the window and door. Both were tightly shut.

"This is what Doig preached! What Madge believed would come to pass!" he cried hoarsely.

There was a strange look of terror in his eyes.

"Julie the housekeeper will have gone, too, if it *is* the—the—"

He did not finish his muttered thought. Like a man walking in his sleep, he moved to the door, opened it, and called loudly, "Julie!"

There came no reply. An eerie stillness was in the house.

He moved on into the kitchen; the room was empty.

He hurried into the garden, calling, "Madge! Julie!" There was no response.

He went back to the house and made a hurried tour of the house. Every room was empty!

He went back to where he had been when Madge

was taken; with a groan he dropped into his chair, staring into space with horror-stricken eyes.

Suddenly, as though a living voice uttered them, the words of scripture sounded in his ears:

"Lest, when I have preached to others, I myself should become disqualified."

A mortal agony filled his eyes as he groaned, "God help me! I know now that I have only been a *minister* by training and by profession; I have never been a son of God by conversion by the new birth!"

His untaught soul had misinterpreted the real inwardness of that passage of Paul's. But it was true; in the sense *he* meant it, he *was* "disqualified."

Chapter 27

❧

A Stricken City

It was not really until business time next morning that London, that the whole country, really fully awoke to the fact of the great event of the previous night. Suburbanites, in many cases, only heard the strange news on their arrival at their particular railway stations. Even then, a hundred rumors were the order of the moment. There were a few rank unbelievers of the garbled stories of the translation who laughed skeptically then began to grumble at the strange disorganization of the railway traffic.

The tens and hundreds of thousands, the millions, poured into London as usual. But the snap had gone out of most of them. A horrible sense of foreboding was upon the spirits of the travelers. As the newspapers more fully confirmed the news, London approached perilously near the verge of a general panic.

The newspapers were bought up with phenomenal

eagerness. There were weather prophecies, political prophecies, financial prophecies, social prophecies—but no prophecy of the coming of the Christ.

The Courier's rival had a brief note to the effect:

> Some wild, senseless rumors were abroad in London last night, as to the sudden, mysterious disappearance of numbers of the ultrareligious persons of London and elsewhere. Some people talked wildly of the end of the world. We therefore dispatched special commissioners to ascertain what truth there was in all this.
>
> Our representatives returned an hour and a half later, after having visited all the chief places of amusement and principal restaurants, but everywhere managers told the same story, "There have been no signs of the end of the world in our place. We are fuller than ever."

But the note of *The Courier*'s clarion call had no uncertain sound. Besides all that we have already seen written in the office by the translated Tom Hammond, and afterward by Ralph Bastin, the latter had added to his postscript another. It was a solemn, pathetic word, and ran as follows:

> Our sheets must go to press in a few moments, if *The Courier* is to be in the

hands of its readers at the usual hour. But before we print, I feel compelled to add a word or two more to what I wrote two hours ago.

During the last two hours, I have made many discoveries, not the least of which is the fact that the nearest and dearest being to my own heart and life is missing. She has shared in the glory and joy of the wondrous, mysterious translation.

I have no wish to parade my own personal griefs before my readers, but dare to say that no journalist ever worked with a more broken, crushed sense of life than did I during the two hours I spent in searching London for facts.

One curious fact that I speedily discovered was that no one had been taken in this wondrous translation from any of the theaters or music halls. In the days before this awfully solemn event, discussions arose periodically in certain religious and semireligious journals as to whether *true* Christians could attend the theater and music hall.

The fact that no one appears to have been translated from any of these London houses of amusement answers, *I* think, that question as it has never been answered before.

Here followed a brief outline of his experiences in other quarters. Then in big black type he asked the question:

WHAT FOLLOWS THIS STUPENDOUS EVENT?— The Bible evidently told those who have been taken from our midst that this translation was approaching; then it must surely give some hint of what we may expect to follow. The questions is, *what* follows?

There must surely be many clergymen and ministers who knew *about* this great translation, who though not living in the spirit of what they knew and being left behind like those of us who were carelessly ignorant—there must be many such ministers left who could teach us what to expect next, and how to prepare for the next eruption—whatever form it may take.

We therefore propose to any such ministers that they gather us into every hall, church, chapel, Salvation Army barracks, or even in the great open spaces and teach us who are left behind how to be prepared for the next mighty change.

Meanwhile, are there no houses in Paternoster Row, and its neighborhood, where books and pamphlets on these momentous subjects can be obtained, or are all such publishers translated with those of whom we have been writing?

One effect of that last suggestion was to send thousands of people to Paternoster Row. Some of the publishers of books on the Lord's second coming *had* been left behind, had *not* shared in the Rapture of which they had printed and published.

Storekeepers, packers, masters, clerks were reading the contents of their own wares. A business system, at first, seemed an unknown quantity. Deadness, amazement, fear, uncertainty, all of these things held and dominated them.

But they had to wake up. Their counters were besieged. Hordes of people thronged the doors. In twenty minutes after the first great influx, there was not a tract, a booklet, or a volume on the Lord's coming and the events to follow left in the "Row."

At any other time those in command of the stores would have tried to get the printing presses to run off some hundreds of thousands of the briefest of the "second advent" literature. But today, fear held everyone in its clutches.

Business everywhere was at a standstill. By eleven o'clock most of the city houses were closed. Some of the banks never opened at all. Throgmorton Street and the Stock Exchange were in a state of dazed incredulity. A few members were missing, and these were known to be "expectants" of the translation.

A dense mass of men and women was marching up the street. Every face was set and serious. There were many clergymen and ministers in the crowd, if the clerical collar and ministerial garb gave true indication of their calling.

"To St. Paul's! To St. Paul's!" a stentorian voice was shouting.

The stockbrokers joined the mighty crowd that swept on.

❧

By midnight, or soon after, only a few hours after the great translation, the hordes of the vicious that festered in the slums had heard something of what had happened, and creeping from their filthy lairs, began at once to become a menace to public life and property.

Many of the police beats were unprotected, the men who had been patrolling them sharing in the sudden glorious rapture of their Lord's return. By midnight, the whole police service had become temporarily disorganized, if not actually demoralized.

Scotland Yard heads of departments were missing, as well as local superintendents, sergeants, etc. In many cases there was no one to give orders or to maintain control. And where leaders *were* left, they were often too scared and unnerved to exercise a healthful authority.

Under these circumstances the hordes grew bolder every hour. They had no fear of the spiritual character of the strange situation, for God, to them, was a name only to blaspheme. Hell was a merry jest to them, a synonym for warmth and rest. Besides, hell had no shadow of terror to people who, for years, had suffered the torments of a life in a literal hell in London.

Shops and private houses and some of the larger business houses had been openly robbed. A rumor got out that the banks were to be raided.

Ralph Bastin, passing the Bank of England, found that the guard of soldiers had been quadrupled, and this for the daytime. The thought that filled his mind was of the strange mood that had suddenly come over everyone; since today everybody seemed ready to talk freely of religious things.

He moved on up Cheapside, his destination being St. Paul's Cathedral.

Chapter 28

❧

IN ST. PAUL'S

The cathedral was packed out to the doors. The aisles and every other inch of standing room were a solid jam. The whole area of the interior showed one black mass of silent, waiting, expectant people.

The great organ was silent. No one dreamed of singing. The choir seats were full of strangers. The stalls were filled with an indiscriminate crowd. There was no rule, no discipline today.

Suddenly the tall, square-built form of a certain well-known bishop rose near the pulpit. He had linked his arm in that of one of London's most popular Nonconformist preachers and almost dragged him to his feet.

There was evidently a controversy going on between the two men as to which of them should address the people, each urging the other to lead off. The same thought was in the minds of nearly all who were in view of the pair, namely, *How comes it that a bishop and a popular preacher like the Rev. Smith have been left behind?*

A deepening silence settled upon the mighty mass gathered under that great dome. Suddenly the silence was broken by a voice calling: "Bishop Haversham."

Another voice immediately cried, "No! The Rev. Smith."

A momentary clamor of voices ensued. The voices were not shrill in their eagerness but sullen, somber, almost savage. A moment later the bishop slowly entered the pulpit. He bowed his head in prayer.

Like the slow, rushing sound of the letting loose of some distant water, the noise of thousands of bending forms filled the place, for everyone bowed the head.

A moment later, the heads were raised. The voice of the bishop broke the silence, crying, "Men and women of London, fellows with me in the greatest shame the world has ever known—the shame of bearing the name Christian, and yet of being the rejected of Christ—we meet today under awful, solemn circumstances.

"We are face-to-face with the most solemnly awful situation the human race has ever known, if we except the conditions under which, during those three hours of blackness at Calvary, the people of Jerusalem were found, while the crucified Christ hung midair on the fatal tree.

"It may be said that our position bears some

likeness to that of the people who were destroyed by the flood. Those antediluvians had one hundred and twenty years' warning; we, as professing Christians, have had nearly two thousand years' warning, yet London, England, and the whole world has by last night's events been proven practically heathen—or atheist.

"The moment came when God called Noah and his family into the ark. But what never occurred to me, until this morning, was the significant fact that God did not shut the door of the ark, or send the flood, until *seven days later*, thus giving the unbelievers another opportunity to be saved.

"And God has given the world this same extra opportunity of being prepared for the return of the Lord and the translation of His Church.

"For some years now, conferences and conventions, addresses, Bible readings, etc., where this subject of the second coming of Christ has been specially taught, have been multiplied mightily. I have been present at some of these gatherings, but smiling amusedly at what I termed the wild utterances of visionaries, I neglected my opportunity.

"Yet of all men, *I* ought to have been prepared for this coming of the Lord. I have held ministerial office in a church that taught the doctrine plainly. But I see now that all through my life, I have been blinded by the *letter* of things and have mistaken christening, confirmation, and communicating for conversion and life in Christ.

"I see today that I entered the established Church of this realm and not the family of God and the service of Christ. I have never really been God's by the new birth, until last night, when my dear wife, in company with all the waiting, longing Church, was suddenly called up to be with her Lord. I was in the room when she disappeared. And I, a professed servant of Christ, was *left*.

"With shame and regret, I have to say to you now that I *ought* to have known the truth and have been prepared, but because I was unconverted, I failed to apprehend the fact of the Lord's near return."

Visible emotion checked the bishop's speech for a moment. Recovering himself, he went on: "A blind leader of the blind, because unborn of God. I *ought* to have known that Christ's return was near. I *should* have known it, if I had been spiritually minded.

"Since last night, I have lived a whole lifetime. I have read the whole of the Gospels and Epistles, and taking my true place as a lost soul before God, I have been born of God. And now, here, in this solemn moment, I bring to you the Spirit-taught knowledge that has been given to me."

For a few minutes, he traversed ground already covered in these pages, then, continuing, he said, "Now let us face our present position, as those who are left! What is the future to be? This is what you need to know, what I need to know! First, the next thing for each to do is to seek the Lord, to cry unto Him for mercy and pardon, while all our hearts are shocked and startled and our thoughts are turned toward God. For unless we become God's and live out the future for Him, our portion will be an eternal hell.

"One thing appears very plain from scripture, that is, that when last night Christ came into the air and caught up His Church, living and dead, the devil, who has been the prince of the power of the air, had to descend to earth. Christ and Beelzebub can never live together in the same realm.

"Now, beloved, the Spirit of God has left the earth. The devil has taken up his abode here with all his myriad agents, and he is going to make earth as hot for those of us who will witness for God as is hell itself to the lost.

"If we will witness for God during the years we are beginning today—called the years of 'The Great Tribulation,' they will probably be seven in number and extend therefore to the dawning moment of the millennium—if we witness, therefore, for God during these intervening seven years, we may expect to meet with hideous trial and suffering.

"Antichrist will now soon make himself known, he will mislead the Jews, who will now return to their own land and build their new temple. For a time, Antichrist will appear to be the friend of the Jews, but he will seek to force the most awful idolatry upon them. The mass of Jewry will accept all this.

"With the Jew, every Gentile will be compelled to accept Antichrist and the Roman Beast. The devil will be so mad at being cast down out of heaven and because he knows he has such a limited time to work against God, that he will call up all hell to stamp out God's people."

For one instant the bishop paused. He leaned over the pulpit edge, his eyes full of the light of a holy determination, but into his voice there crept a tender yearning as he continued: "Are we prepared for actual martyrdom? For this will certainly be the fate of many who will not bear upon them the mark of the Beast."

The most solemn hush rested upon the vast mass of people as the bishop returned to his seat.

Chapter 29

❧

Conclusion

Quietly, giving the impression that the sense of a great shame rested upon him, the Rev. Smith rose from his seat and faced the congregation. Everyone waited breathlessly, wondering what contribution he would make to the great matter at hand.

"God help me, dear friends!" he began. "For I know now that I have been a Judas to the Lord of life and glory, whose *professed* servant I have been. I have gloried in my success; in the crowd that always filled my church; in the adulation of my intellectual powers by the press. But I have never glorified Christ. In a hundred subtle ways I have denied my Lord—He *is* my Lord *now*; I have found Him in the silence of the past awful night. I have been practically denying His deity for years; I have talked learnedly when I ought to have been walking humbly, and—and—"

The strain was too much for him; tears streamed down his face, and he covered his face with his hands and dropped, sobbing, into his seat.

Sobs broke from many of the people. In another moment the released pent-up emotions would have become a storm that no one could have stayed. But the bishop's voice called out, "Let us pray!"

Every head was bent, and a prayer, such as London's Cathedral had never heard before, poured from the bishop's lips. The conclusion of the prayer was followed by a moment or two of deepest stillness.

From outside, in the street, there suddenly arose the roar of a multitude, crying, "Fire!" Fortunately, the packed congregation within the cathedral realized that the alarming thing was *out*side, not *in*side, the building, so there was no panic.

In a few minutes the great place was cleared. The bishop, the great Nonconformist, and a dozen other ministers and laymen remained gathered together, as by a common instinct, by the pulpit.

"What is coming, brethren?"

"The power of Antichrist and the manifestation of the man of sin himself," cried the bishop solemnly.

A week later. . .

Like a sow that returns to the mud, the world had returned to its old careless life. The fever for sport, pleasure, money making, drinking, gambling, licentiousness was fiercer than ever. Everyone aimed at forgetting what had happened a week before.

There had been many conversions during the first forty-eight hours after the translation of the Church, but since then, scarcely one. Already there had arisen, all over the world, as the press telegrams made clear, a multitude of men and women who were preaching the maddest, most dangerous doctrines.

Among the most popular and successful of these was Spiritualism. Not the comparatively mild form known *before* the great translation, but a hideous, blasphemous exhibition that proved itself to be what it had really always been—*demonology*.

Antichrist's sway had begun. Satan was a positive, active agent. The restraints of the Holy Spirit were missing, for He had left the earth when the Church had been taken away. Other restraints were also taken from the midst of the people, since the fact remains, whether the world recognized it or not, that the people of God are the salt, the preservative of the earth.

Look for All of the FAITH CLASSICS from Barbour Publishing

Barbour's Faith Classics offer compelling, updated text and an easy-reading typesetting, all in a fresh new trim size. Introduce a new generation to these books worth reading!

Confessions by Saint Augustine

The God of All Comfort by Hannah Whitall Smith

Grace Abounding by John Bunyan

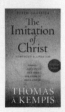

The Imitation of Christ by Thomas à Kempis

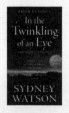

In the Twinkling of an Eye by Sydney Watson

Quiet Talks on Prayer by S.D. Gordon

Each title: Paperback / 4.1875" x 7.5" / 192 pages

Available wherever Christian books are sold.